Issue Four

Editors
Ginny Baily and Sally Flint

Front Cover Image
Matt Thomas

Printed by imprintdigital.net Exeter

Published 2009 by Dirt Pie Press

The Editors would like to acknowledge the support of the Creative Writing and Arts Department at the University of Exeter and thank members of the editorial board for their assistance with this volume.

www.riptidejournal.co.uk

ISBN 978-0-9558326-2-8

Contents

Introduction

Jane Feaver

John Cheever described the short story as the literature of the nomad. In 'those rented summer houses, those one-night love affairs, and those lost key rings' he says, we might find a 'newness', something which confounds 'traditional esthetics' [sic].

Architecturally, compared to the novel's grandiose constructions, the short story is a tent. There are many advantages to the form, not least, a refusal to settle down and a pragmatism that extends not only to the practical but – as Cheever noted – to the moral. Unless we are to sit with water trickling down our collars, the structure must be, at least for the duration, every bit as robust; but it can afford to be more carefree, not so deeply embedded in the ground. Cheever sees the distinction as one of responsibility: the novel, 'in all its greatness', he says, is still having to pay attention to the Classical unities, 'preserving that mysterious link between esthetics and moral fitness'.

By contrast, the short story is ideally equipped to capture the ephemeral, the arbitrary, the dubious, the unfit-for-service – those perversely ordinary moments so often overlooked, by which the majority of us live out our lives.

What unites the stories in this fourth volume of Riptide – a journal that over the past few years has provided a wonderful haven for the form, is an ability to set up camp quickly in the unlikeliest of places. This gathering is geographically, historically, socially and culturally diverse, yet there is a touching sociability as the narratives stand together cheek by jowl, and a remarkable openness across their differences. Wherever they take us, there is a sense of summer slipping away.

Whether it be encounters in rural Ireland or deepest Colombia, a municipal park or the foothills of the Alps, or, indeed, a fetid flat, in which under any other circumstances, we would prefer not to venture, these stories flirt with and quiz the questions that concern us all: Where are we from? Who are we? Where are we? What are our real taboos?

It is time, they seem to be saying, to grasp the moment and to savour the last rays of the sun while we can.

The Voice, the Fish Woman and the Coconut Girlie

Joel Willans

Out in the ocean, toward the horizon, some surfer rides this wall-sized wave. Nearer the shore, the sparkling heads of swimmers dive and surface; nearer still, at the ocean's edge, boys and girls unsure of the water wade in slowly, daring each other forward. And then, on a blue and white beach towel far from water, there's me, sweating as I hug my knees.

I watch the surfer skim across the wave. He flips his board one way then the other, toying with the surge of green-blue water as if aware that every woman on the beach must be watching him; just when it seems he's tamed it and will ride it home, it catches him. His board spears the sky and all I see is his body falling into the fizzing white froth.

That's life, I think. That's your life, the voice in my head says. It's right. It's always right.

I return to my study of the girl sunbathing near me. I try to laze back, adjust my sunglasses and hope against hope I look cool. She is only five yards away, this girl. Her hair is piled up in a soft black curl; her body shining with oil is covered by a stripy yellow-green bikini that is held together with nothing more than colourful bits of string.

Five yards away and yet it feels so far. I'll not leave until I speak to her. Any minute now I'll ask her for a light. I don't normally smoke in the day, definitely not in this heat. But she's smoking, this beach goddess, and that's my way in. The cigarette I have been twirling through my fingers is all buckled and dirty, stained with sun-tan lotion, so I toss it aside and pull another from my packet.

Get real, says the voice in my head.

Thing is, this time I am real. It's all about timing. I'm a devout believer in this. If I time it right, she might say 'yeah sure I've got a light' and then she might ask where I'm from and do I fancy meeting up later in this cute little beach bar she knows with star-shaped lamps and cocktails the size of flower pots.

Dream on, the voice says. Yeah, I do, I almost shout. I dream a lot. I can fly with this as far as I like. We're on holiday in Mexico. Now we're in Copenhagen, drinking in a harbour bar. Now we're trashing the snowman we built to save it from the slow death of thawing. She's glowing with the cold, and she's laughing.

First, I need to speak to her. That's all I need to do. But there's a problem here; I can't see her eyes. Not only is she looking out across the ocean, she's wearing these big wraparound shades that hide half her face. I need to see her eyes before I can make my move. For all I know, she is gawping at one of those pumped-up boys slicing across the sea on their boards. This thought makes me snap my cigarette in half and grind it into the sand.

One of the surfers ambles past me. He is all pecs and tattoos, all bracelets and dreadlocks. If he weren't carrying a surfboard, you'd think he was just a hippie with a tan. A hippie with a tan and a six-pack. He has no beer gut. None. I'm not a big drinker, but when I look down there are a couple of little baby rolls of fat. Staring at my belly, those little rolls shining with coconut suntan lotion, I get that dizzy feeling again.

I know it well. It's almost as frequent a companion as the voice. Apparently this feeling is the beginning of the downward spiral: that's how the doctor described it, as though the loathing that fills me is some sort of sadistic fairground ride. Think positive, he said, you're a young man with plenty to offer. I repeat this phrase, the way he told me to. I'm a young man with plenty to offer. Plenty to offer.

Yeah, the voice says. To liposuction professionals, maybe. I sigh and ease myself up from the sand. There's a whining in my head as I stand up, and my legs feel good to buckle.

Loser, the voice says. Loser. I clench my fists and wait to see if it has any other words of wisdom for me, but for now it stays quiet. I know it's right. It always is. It told me I was shit at my job and should leave before they fired me, and it told me that Bella was too good for me and was playing around with my flatmate. It's so damn smug, knowing everything, but then it's easy for it to chirp away with these simple truths. It doesn't have to deal with the things I have to deal with.

Even with my eyes closed, the sunlight makes everything orange. I take a deep breath and hold it for a count of ten. Then slowly I exhale. It's a technique taught by my old sales trainer, it was meant to prepare us for big presentations. Of course that's not something I need to worry about any more, but it does the job and I feel my body relax. Opening my eyes I see that the girl has turned round and seems to be looking directly at me.

I want to run away. I want to bury myself in the sand. Instead, and God knows why, I look over her head as if I haven't even seen her, stick out my arms and attempt to do some Tai Chi thing with my hands. Weaving them between each other, I imagine that I'm dancing at a club and slowly playing with the strobes.

What the hell do you look like, the voice says. She's going to think you're a right twat.

I don't know if it's the power of the sun or the sound of the sea or both, but I manage to ignore it. When, eventually, she looks the other way, I drop to my knees, sweating more than I have all day.

I know life wasn't always like this, but when I try to remember how it was before, it's like trying to recall a film I watched when I'd had too much to drink. It's pointless dwelling on the past, that's another of the doctor's classics, but sometimes the present is just so tiring. I have an overwhelming urge to curl up in a ball and nuzzle the sand, or to walk steadily into the sea. The voice usually keeps quiet if I stay still and do nothing. I could maybe just sit here and carry on watching the girl. The thought makes me blush. Perhaps I should just go to bed, neck a couple of pills and wait for tomorrow.

'Buy ma biscuits or kiss ma fish! Buy ma biscuits or kiss ma fish!'

For a second, I think it's the voice, messing around with me. So, when I spot a woman waddling across the beach, a box stuffed with cookies balanced on her head and a dead puffer fish in her hand, I grin. She wears a yellow smock so bright it looks like her dark head is fixed to a body made of gold. I must be staring, because she flashes me a big grin. I smile back.

'Wanna kiss my fish?' she says.

I shake my head, gazing at the dead thing she swings in front of my face. It looks like a grey football with fat lips and spikes. 'I'm not that desperate.' I say.

She laughs. Her chin wobbles. 'Then you gotta buy my biscuits. That's the deal. Biscuit or fish, your choice.'

The smell of that rotting fish is making me gag. 'What if I don't want either?'

'Listen, junior. Sometimes life gives you difficult choices. So you can kiss this or eat one of these. That's not difficult, is it?' She shows me a biscuit with chocolate chunks big as pennies

'What other flavours have you got?'

'I got choccy, I got coconut, I got cinnamon. I got everything.'

Over her shoulder I can see the girl. She has taken her glasses off and is looking at us. She has eyes green as glass, almost too big for her face.

I lean closer to the woman.' What do you think that girl over there would like?'

The woman glances round. 'She's a coconut girlie. For sure.'

'You reckon?'

'I know a coconut girlie when I see one, and she one all over.'

She doesn't know shit, the voice says.

'Okay,' I say. 'Give me one coconut.'

My hand shakes as I pass her the money. She grabs my palm in hers. I'm surprised how soft it is. 'You don't need to get yourself in a tizzy. I tell you she's a coconut girlie then she is,' she says, giving my hand a squeeze.

She doesn't know what she is talking about, the voice shouts. Wake up. Sit down. The voice makes me jump. It's loud, angry.

The woman stares into my eyes. 'Listen, junior, if she ain't a coconut girlie, I'll kiss ma own fish. Right here, in front of the whole damn beach.'

The girl is still watching us. I take a deep breath and take a step towards her. You're going to bottle it, the voice says. I hold the coconut biscuit flat upon my palm, and now the ache comes, twisting my stomach. I bite my lip and take two more steps. The girl is staring at me, not smiling, not anything.

You look like a loser, the voice says. I shake my head trying to shut it up; another step, and then I freeze. It's as far as I can go. It's good enough, I think. I tried. I did something. The girl starts to turn away. Yes, the voice says, you did well. Now sit down and be quiet.

'Remember, I'll kiss it, I'm gonna kiss it for you!' the woman shouts.

Hearing her, I stumble forward and I'm there by the girl's side. She looks up at me. I swallow hard. I wish I'd never bothered, wish I'd just gone back to my room, blacked out the windows and sunk into bed. Now it's too late. I will humiliate myself again. I want to throw the biscuits at the woman, but instead I hold out the cookie. Crumbs drop through my fingers.

'Do you like coconut?' I say.

'What?' the girl says

'Do you – I thought you liked coconut?'

She looks at the biscuit and then looks me up and down and I'm waiting for the sand to cave in and the sea to wash me away. I want to punch myself for being so fucking stupid and the doctor for telling me to take a little break and the woman for saying she will kiss her fish. Then her hand reaches towards mine, and with delicate fingers she plucks the cookie from my palm. She smiles.

'Yeah, as it happens. How did you know?' she says.

I shrug. 'I just knew.'

'I'll share it with you if you want?'

I nod and drop to my knees, though my mouth is too dry to eat. The woman shuffles past, swinging her fish. She waves it at me and I smile back again. It feels like my face has set with this huge stretching smile. My mouth hurts with the strength of it. Even when a surf boy struts past, it doesn't go away. I wait for the voice to tell me that I look like a prick, that the girl will think I'm a fucking moron if I don't stop grinning like a clown and say something to her. But she's eating the cookie, and I'm still smiling, and the voice doesn't say a single word.

Sammy

Nicholas Hogg

When he was there and not being chased by teachers over the back fields, Nigsy was the only black kid at school.

Before I knew anything about race and colour, I knew that calling him Nigsy was wrong. Not because of some historical understanding of slaves and oppression and chained men on ships – I was only ten – but because my mum's boyfriend would say nigger this and nigger that at every opportunity. And what I did know was that what came out of his mouth was pretty much bollocks. One time at the dinner table, when mum was in the kitchen, he thought he'd tell me and my brother a joke.

'What do you throw a drowning Paki?'

Both of us had heard it before but said nothing.

'A brick.'

My little brother laughed and I kicked him under the table and we carried on eating our chips or something like a Findus Crispy Pancake.

Anyway, I was about to tell you about me and Sammy, because that was his name. Not that many kids called him by it. They mostly didn't say Nigsy to his face, either. He was a proper bad boy, and this was in the day of corporal punishment when teachers could throw right hooks and crack your knuckles open with wooden rulers. I took some blows myself, but nothing compared to Sammy. Shit, how many times did I see his head rocking back and forth with whack from a dinner lady or the PE teacher.

'I don't give a toss,' he'd say, returning from a pasting in the head's office. 'Me old man hits harder than he does.' He wasn't lying about that, not with all those cuts and bruises. Eleven years old and his skin was already a map of scars.

This one afternoon, no-one was getting smacked. It

was near the end of term, one of those June days when a teacher daydreams about their summer holidays and thinks, *fuck it*, and calls off the lesson to take the class outside and play rounders or read books.

Or make kites.

Me and Sammy paired up. We all got green sticks and a big sheet of coloured paper. Once everyone had their stuff, Sammy went round and made sure we had the longest and straightest sticks.

'Bet we're making the biggest kite.'

Other kids cut their sheets of paper in half and listened to the teacher, Mr Fallon, using rulers to measure off the corners and fold in the right places. While they were following his instructions I was taping two sticks together and Sammy was drawing portholes with cartoon soldiers inside. In no time a couple of the girls, Debs and Jan, launched their little kite into the blue. They even had some daisies tied on the tail.

'Tails are wet.'

Sammy agreed.

We got on with it, using more Sellotape than everyone else put together. And soon enough we had the roll to ourselves as most of the class were setting their kites on the wind. When we were finally done, Sammy took the kite and I had the string. We ran the length of that field, a fair stretch of grass before they sold the top end off for a housing estate, but our kite didn't get much higher than the dandelions.

'You're not running fast enough,' shouted Sammy, again throwing the kite up hard, in the hope it would stay there.

'You do it then.'

So Sammy ran, and that crappy kite of tape and garden sticks twisted and turned, jerked skyward, then swerved either left or right before crashing into the ground.

I went to pick it up again and Sammy carried on yanking it.

'Stop pulling it.'

'Throw the fucker properly, then.'

Mr Fallon probably heard the swearing but let it go, glad to have Sammy doing something he was supposed to be and not making ninja throwing stars from razor blades or chucking some kid in the pond.

'You need a tail,' he told us. 'And the instructions were two sticks, not four.' He held the kite with both hands. 'Blimey, look at the size of it. If it does take off you'll be carried into the sky.'

That comment made us even more determined to make it fly, and we sat down on the grass and got the scissors and more tape. Sammy was twisting newspaper into bows and knotting them into the length of string tied at the base.

'I told you we needed a tail.'

'Did you bollocks. You said they were wet.'

By the time we'd done making the longest tail in the class, the bell rang for the end of school.

'Sir,' begged Sammy. 'Let us fly it. Go on, Sir.'

Mr Fallon was all right considering the little dictators we had as teachers, but he was having none of staying around when he could go home. 'We'll fly it Monday,' he promised.

'What if there's no wind?' I asked, but he wasn't listening. He was walking into the classroom swinging his car keys around his fingers.

'Leave your kites on the bookshelves 'til next week,' he said.

Sammy turned to me and asked, 'You ain't going home, are you?'

'Am I fuck.' Of course I wasn't. It was Friday, a half day for my mum's boyfriend. He'd be on the sofa with a beer telling me to shut up if I made any noise while he was watching telly. He hadn't been around long, so he hadn't hit me yet, but I knew it was coming.

'What about Wurzel?'

Wurzel was the caretaker, padlocking the gates after all the kids had gone.

'We'll go under the hedge when he starts walking back to his house.'

It was a good idea. He lived at the front, so once you were on the back field he couldn't see you.

We sat on the kerb while the kids came out of school, some of the older ones walking home on their own, the nippers getting met by childminders and mums, or some of the dads with no jobs.

When two of the older girls from our class, Steph and Katie, were far enough down the street to guess Sammy wasn't going to chase them, they sang, '*Nigsy's kite is shit, Nigsy's kite is shit.*'

He picked up a stone and hurled it. They ran. 'Dogs.'

We watched Wurzel wobble over and lock the gates, sliding a heavy chain between the rails. 'You two up to no good by the looks of it.'

'Just sitting.'

'I bet you are. If I catch you messing around in here you'll be taking a cane from the headmaster come Monday.'

We shuffled away a bit to give the impression of respect. Then once he got back to his house, we ducked through a gap in the hedge and sprinted across the front playground.

School after hours was always a bit freaky. The quiet, empty classrooms. All our stuff pinned on the walls looked strange now, pictures of Normans and Saxons, giraffes and lions, collages made of rotting leaves. And no one shouting or crying, no teachers telling you to get back to work or sit properly on a plastic chair. We cupped our hands and looked in the windows. I don't know if Sammy had the same feeling, but when I thought about it I could see us sat there earlier that day, or perhaps a day not even happened yet.

'Come on,' he said. 'In case the wind drops.'

We walked onto the back field, surrounded by pastures filled with black and white cows. Though if you looked over the fence on the right you could see a half-built estate, the empty shells waiting for more kids like us. If they were coming at all, because we could've been the last two boys on earth it was that quiet.

'Chuck it up, then,' shouted Sammy. 'And I'll run.'

I did. And this time that crappy kite was fantastic. It flew. It put a shape in an empty sky.

'Look at it fly.' Sammy was jumping and leaping. 'How high do you reckon that is?'

When I told him it was my turn I thought there might be a bit of a problem, but Sammy passed me the string and chased the kite shadow racing across the grass.

'Make it go higher,' he screamed.

'The string's right out.'

'I wish we had more.'

My mum had a reel of thick cotton in the sink cupboard that said on the label, "A Mile of Cotton." I told Sammy.

'Bullshit.'

'That's what it says. A whole mile long.'

'That'd be far out!'

'I'll run home and get it.'

'Won't your dad make you stop in if he sees you?'

'He ain't me dad for a start.'

'Keep yer hair on mate.'

'He's a twat. I hate it when people think he's me old man.'

Sammy was tugging on the kite, jerking it up and down. 'Least you can say he ain't your proper dad.'

'See you in five minutes.'

'Don't get caught.'

'And don't mess the kite up.'

Halfway down the field I looked back and Sammy was sat on the fence. A boy and a kite. I never saw him as peaceful as that again.

*

It was a proper mission to get this cotton, because once I was home, I was supposed to wait till mum got back. Since her boyfriend started coming round early on Fridays I had to leave the back door key for him under the milk bottle holder. Usually I stayed at the childminders with my little brother, because if it was only us in the house someone might call the Social. But on Fridays I was allowed to make toast and watch telly. Not that I wanted to hang around with you-know-who.

So, I slipped down the gap between our garage and the neighbour's. I knew he was in because his boots were outside and I guessed he was watching a Western because it sounded like a gunfight in the lounge. How loud he had the volume up I could've put my fist through the glass and he wouldn't have heard, probably thought it was the saloon window shot out.

Anyway, the door was unlocked. I lowered the handle, crept over the lino and opened up the sink cupboard. I lifted that giant reel of cotton and ran all the way back to school without stopping.

*

I ran up the back field waving it above my head. Sammy was pretty much where I left him, the kite swinging on the breeze, that tail of old news whipping below.

'Look,' I showed him the label.

He read slowly. Although he was in the top year, he was in some special reading class with younger kids.

'A whole mile.'

But he knew what it said all right, and started hauling the kite in so we could get it tied on, asking me if a mile was higher than the clouds.

I wasn't sure. 'We might hit a plane, though.'

'That'd be mental.'

I got the cotton tied nice and tight.

'Make sure you double the knot,' advised Sammy. 'I'd hate for us to lose it.'

'I'll treble it.'

And once I had, she was away, running out that reel like a fish would a line. Sammy was jubilant. He gave me the reel because he was too excited to hold it, dancing about as the cows in the field watched him jump and shout. The line was spinning out rapidly, and it was cool to watch it unravel.

'How much cotton left?'

'Maybe half?'

Sammy wanted me to let it rip, but if I did it too fast, the kite lost height.

'About three-quarters gone, now.' I passed it over. 'You have a go.'

'Shit,' he said, feeling the tug of all that line strung into the sky. 'It's really heavy.'

'I can hardly see it.'

'Do you reckon if we let the lot out, it'd float over Barkby church?'

From where we stood on the fence, we could see the steeple loom above the wild hedgerows, the copse of oak where rooks nested in the higher branches. Beyond all this was an old manor house, and only on a clear day like that one could you see it floating on the heat shimmer.

'Let it all out,' I said.

And Sammy did, till that kite made of garden sticks, rolled up newspaper and too much tape was a speck of red. It was that far away you had to follow the cotton to find where it was.

'Shit.'

Until the cotton ran off the reel, and left just the naked plastic in Sammy's hands.

'Get it.'

I jumped down into the field, but it was gone, flown. The last thing I saw was a wisp of black cotton pulled into the sky.

'I can't even see the kite,' said Sammy. 'Where is it?'

It had been so high it seemed impossible for it to have fallen so quickly. But it had vanished.

'Maybe it got carried higher,' I said. 'Went up instead of down.'

Sammy was staring into the distance. 'I tell you, that kite was brilliant.'

We walked about the long grass a bit more, looking for the cotton until the cows got curious and started wandering over and spooking us out.

'Piss off,' snapped Sammy, picking up lumps of dried mud, and probably their own shit, and lobbing it at them.

We sat down on the other side of the fence on the school field, twisting up dandelions and talking. Stuff about how far the kite might have flown, whether birds would attack if it was still floating on the wind. We were talking about the kite to delay the fact it was finished, gone.

About an hour later the police came.

We ran, even though all we were doing was sitting around a fire we'd lit in one of the lofts on the building site, poking the flames and pretending we had burgers grilling, looking at the sky through bare rafters, not talking about the kite, but still thinking about it flying over another town.

I'll never forget the cop cars screeching up that driveway, or being chased down the brook, and how I very nearly crapped myself when I heard they had a dog.

I'll never forget what Sammy said in that loft.

'I ain't going home tonight.' He'd kicked the fire some more with his foot. 'I'd rather live here.' He pulled a flame out on the end of a stick and watched it closely, his dark eyes huge in the flickering glow. I could see the scald marks around his mouth where his dad had once poured in boiling water. Just when I thought he might cry he looked at me and said, 'Be a better laugh if you run away, too.'

I looked at the sun going down on that construction site, the scaffolding and bricks, some houses finished with fresh turf for a lawn, others just walls or footings. Nothing either of us knew about life in a house like that was something we wanted.

I said, 'Let's run across the fields to Barkby.'

But we never did, because someone saw smoke and called a fire engine and a squad car, flashing blue lights.

Once the police had taxied me home and lectured me in the lounge, taking off their hats and declining cups of tea, mum cried and took the washing out to hang in the garden. Then my mum's boyfriend came into my bedroom and said, 'If I hear you're hanging about with that nigger kid again you'll feel more than the back of my hand.'

The thing is, it was only when someone else mentioned it I even remembered he was black. And anyway, I was more bothered by my mum's boyfriend calling Sammy names than his divvy threats. If Sammy hadn't been expelled from secondary school we'd have carried on being mates. Best mates, even. He hit a teacher, if I remember. Though it all started before that, the anger and the running, how he'd sprint those back fields.

*

That was some time ago now. When I was last in town I heard he'd been banged up again. Dealing and burglary, various assault charges. He might have outrun the teachers and his old man, occasionally the police, but they all caught up with him in the end. From what I can work out, he's spent as much of his life in the nick as he has free.

Whatever 'free' means.

Maybe it means something like tying a kite to a mile of cotton. Or the memory of it, tugging at the wind and pulling us skyward, then snapping the line and flying.

Bhai and the Manager

Anita Sivakumaran

Bhai surveys Bangalore City from the back seat of his big, white Cielo. He looks at his wrist watch. It is still early. Chandni won't be on stage for at least an hour. He taps on Mithun's shoulder. Mithun turns and says, 'Yes Bhai?'

'Keep your eyes on the road. Pointing your ears toward me is enough.'

Mithun turns to the road, honks generously and generally, then turns his eyes again on Bhai and says, 'Yes Bhai.'

It's no use. It's this same mulishness that makes him an efficient and dedicated lieutenant. 'Take me for a round. Jayanagar to Cox town.'

The traffic is atrocious as ever. A string of eight-seater Qualis cars cut from the left, the drivers with their palms clamped on the horns. Mithun honks back furiously, but their sound is louder. The bloody call-centre kids being driven to work.

One of the Qualis sudden-brakes in front of the Cielo, and even though Mithun swerves to the left, the Cielo's fender rams sideways into the back of the Qualis. Shrill of glass. Mithun halts the car.

The Qualis driver jumps out and, seeing his backlight broken, advances to Mithun's window. Shaking a fist and mouthing obscenities, he taps on it. Mithun turns to Bhai for permission to act. Bhai says, 'Wait,' and winds down his window. The driver turns. Bhai looks at him evenly and says, 'Do you have a problem?'

The driver's face splits into an uneasy grin and he stammers, 'No, no problem. Salaam Bhai, I'll be on my way,' and he runs to his car and drives off.

Mithun gets out and checks the fender. 'No damage,' he says to Bhai.

They carry on. Daily he encounters such irritations. They overwhelm him. His visits to the dance bar to see Chandni are what sustain him. For nothing much else does. His profession is in decline. Kali-yuga is already here, everyone chants, and he can almost believe it, for he is almost a religious man. It has to be the age of Kali, looking at what the city has become in the last five years. Mindless youth working in IT and call centres. Even the college kids have no vigour, no life. Drugs are cheap but the students are into gyms and health-food. Even the prostitution ring is floundering. Men go to bars to pick up women for straight sex, and the women give it up for free. Only the truly depraved require prostitutes.

He can't get into guns, because the Afghans are in charge of that. The Iranians control the passport racket. Within the city, the cops run things with politicians. There isn't any room for Bhai now. What could he run profitably? A game parlour. And it isn't even illegal.

He remembers his upcoming meeting with the manager fellow with dismay. The man insisted this is the only time he could meet. When Bhai told him he had business at the dance bar, the man wanted to come too. They are to have their meeting before Chandni comes on stage. Bhai will make sure.

'Drive to the bar.'

'Bhai?'

He has spoken in Kannada instead of Hindi. He tells Mithun in Hindi to floor it to the dance bar. It's been ten years since Mithun came to Bangalore, and he still cannot understand a word of Kannada. The Deccan plateau could unhinge from the continent, but Mithun would remain exactly where he is. Bhai, on the other hand, whether he likes it or not, has to move and morph according to the times. Hindi, Kannada, English, he speaks them all.

He studies his four gold rings and ten-sovereign bracelet. A college chick told him that gold jewellery isn't cool anymore, or even silver. He was amazed not only by the fact that wearing expensive metal could be seen as 'cheap' but also at the nerve of her. Gold had been his father's business, and the one in which Bhai cut his teeth. Muthappa Rai, kingpin of the Mangalore underworld. Made his fortune by running boats into the little beaches from Mangalore to Goa, half the length of Golconda coast. Nowadays the sons of whores in the government allow people to carry up to five kilograms duty free, and plane tickets are as cheap as plates of masal-dosa. He had given the girl a playful spanking and sent her home with one of his gold chains.

Bhai straightens his silk kurta and checks his hair in the rear view mirror as the car comes to a halt. A khaki-clad parking attendant starts to shoo the car someplace else, but recognising Bhai, he bows and salaams and tries to open the door. Mithun, quick as a snake, jumps out, shoves the man aside and opens the door himself. Only two years ago, the man would've recognised the Cielo from fifty feet away, ordered the traffic to make way for it, even parked it right by the entrance. Now, he offers a spot by the side of the building. Bhai leaves Mithun to deal with the parking and enters the dance bar. Inside, it is all gloom and hush. The music hasn't yet started. The girls haven't begun their dance numbers.

The bar owner ushers Bhai to his table and bawls at a waiter to fetch his drink. His usual table. To the right of the stage with a view of most of the bar, yet close enough to perceive the sheen on Chandni's glossed mouth. His usual drink. Whisky and water. Three parts scotch, the best the bar has, and one part water, plain, still. He no longer has the stomach for neat whisky. There are whispers among his minions that he's losing his stomach for a lot of other strong stuff too. He is a smart man. He has eyes in the back of his head. He's aware of all the rumours.

Mithun comes and sits at the next table. Bhai beckons him over. This man, his rock. Mithun of the old ways, the unchanging ways. His existence a comfort to him nowadays when he is uneasy in his own skin. And it is only a small thing, asking him to sit at his table, a done thing in fact, in these modern times. Mithun would always remember how Bhai had treated him like an equal, sharing his table and drinks. If Mithun put his life on the line for Bhai, it would be for such small considerations.

Bhai looks at his watch. They start the music, a cabaret number from a recent Hindi film.

'That mother-lover, why isn't he here yet?'

'Shall I call him on the cell, Bhai?' Mithun gets to his feet. He wouldn't dare make a phone call in front of Bhai.

'No, sit down, sit down. We will give him another five minutes.'

Mithun sits down and sips his whisky.

'What is this business coming to, eh? We, waiting for some two-bit *manager* son of a whore like he is some daddy.'

'Yes, Bhai,' says Mithun.

Bhai stares at the girl on stage dancing to the tinny number. She shakes her buttocks and flaps her khagra, flashing fat thighs and blackened knees. There is only one other man in the bar apart from Bhai and Mithun and he is staring into his drink.

'My father would turn in his grave to see what is becoming of us,' says Bhai.

'He would, Bhai,' says Mithun and touches his fingers to his eyes and mouth, superstitiously.

In spite of his irritation about the manager being late, there is a tingle in his groin. Delicious-like. His anticipation of Chandni's performance.

For two years he's liked her. Before Chandni, he could have any girl he wanted. And he did, lots of them, but once he had them, it was over. The desire was always only skin-deep, even though he wanted to feel more. He had post-coital depression, every time. Chandni, she's different. He watches her from his dark corner, and sends her anonymous tips. She doesn't know of his existence. He comes here every week, desires her, revels in his desire, but does not speak of it. His liking for her has grown into something overwhelming. All else has lost its meaning: the endless politics, the rage, the fawning minions who respect his position rather than the man he is. The only thing real is his love, yes, why not call it what it is, for this nautch-girl.

There are only ten minutes before Chandni's number is due to begin when the manager-son arrives. But Bhai decides to keep his cool. He needs the lout more than the lout needs him.

The man, with his tie and his steam-pressed shirt, smiles, removes his sunglasses and extends a hand. Bhai looks at it. Nobody shakes hands in his business. Everyone salaams, including Hindus. Well, not all Hindus. The odd Hindu who does a namaste isn't treated any different. The man has a wishy-washy hand. Bhai presses it hard. He could squeeze the bones till they snap. He lets it go.

Mithun disappears into the background as they commence to talk business.

'Do you know how many call-centre employees live in Bangalore?' the man asks.

Bhai waits for the answer.

'Two million,' says the man, as if he were announcing a jackpot.

Bhai nods as though he knew that already.

'And most of them, one point seven million, according to these figures I have,' the man taps his briefcase which is resting on his lap, '*one point seven million*, work nights.'

Bhai nods again.

'And all of them need entertainment in the daytime, continues the man. 'Entertainment with a capital E, when they get out of work in the rush hour school-traffic morning, so they can unwind before they go to bed. Although,' he holds a finger up as if to restrain Bhai from jumping in with a remark, though Bhai is doing nothing of the sort, 'most of them, according to my research,' he knocks on the briefcase again, 'are insomniacs.'

'Is that so?'

'And do you know how many people have savvied up to this fact? None. And how many entertainment venues do you think are available to these one point seven million people? Huhn? Tell me?'

'None?' ventures Bhai.

'Exactly.' The man knuckle-raps the table, grinning his head off.

Bhai steals a look at the stage to see if Chandni has come on. The spotlight brightens and wanes.

The man's gin and tonic arrives. He takes a dainty sip and continues his pitch. 'So you get the picture as it is so far. This is where we come in.'

21

'We do?' Bhai is distracted. The music starts for Chandni's signature number.

The man gets up and moves one place around the table, directly between Bhai and the stage. Fury rises within Bhai; he's unable to see any of the stage, but what can he say? That he wants to watch the dance girl? It would be undignified. He cannot be seen craning his neck around the man to catch a glimpse. There are now ten or fifteen men at the bar. He sees them perk up and knows she's on stage.

The man lays out his plan to conquer the wallets of insomniac call centre employees while the rest of the bar converges closer upon the stage as Chandni gets going with her dance number. Bhai is stuck looking at the man's face as though in rapt attention, thirsting for the odd glimpse of her from around his earlobes or shoulder-tops.

'A casino,' says the man. 'Let the fuckers gamble away their money. You know we don't even have proper night-time casinos in this city, let alone daytime. All this IT money, and no real way to spend it.' He shakes his head.

Bhai, despite his resolution not to show any interest in the man's proposition for the first two meetings, says, 'Tell me more.'

'The USP of course, is that it opens at eight in the morning, for all those people not able to go to bed yet, and with all this money they can't spend in the evenings and weekends because they are bloody working.'

'Tell me one thing,' says Bhai, 'this is a good business idea. Why didn't you go to a bank for a loan?'

The man sits back and sighs. 'You won't believe it,' he says, 'but then I think, you will believe it, otherwise you won't be the alternative source of money eh, niche in the market that you have. The banks,' he pauses dramatically, '*all the banks*, have this in their clause or almanac or something, that they won't loan money to gambling institutions. Not only is it immoral,' he leans forward for the punchline, 'but also, it is too big a gamble.' He laughs uproariously, and two or three of the men tear their eyes away from Chandni to give him a look of annoyance. Then they catch sight of Bhai and hurriedly look away.

The man stops laughing and collects himself. 'Which is why I'm here. You be the funds, I'll be the brains. It's all very legitimate. We'll get the proper licenses. I have contacts in the government who'll sign the papers for one third of what they usually charge. A bargain. And for staff and security, we'll have a combination of your goons and my girls, I know a lot of slick college girls looking for part-time jobs. Your goons, hell, they can go legit by getting proper security jobs eh?' He laughs again.

Bhai senses Mithun flinching in anger. Bhai is in a classic dilemma. The man is a horror, but his idea is top rate. And yes, his *goons* would benefit from a legit job. They are getting blood crazy and restless in their freelance capacity, what with the sluggish state all the usual business is in. He makes his mind up as the man garbles on.

'I had this stroke of inspiration, this masterstroke, then I looked up and thought, what am I doing in this job? I'm more than a Manager, even General Manager, that was my post, as you know. I'm more than that, I'm an entrepreneur with a capital E. Immediately I collected all the figures necessary, and hey presto, here we are in the crucial stage. My wife, she said when I…'

'Listen to me,' Bhai interrupts the man. The man shuts up and waits for Bhai to speak. 'I agree this is a good idea. You can count on my involvement, financially and otherwise.'

The man grins and grabs Bhai's hand, causing Mithun suddenly and menacingly to materialise by his shoulder. 'Deal is deal. We are partners now, Mr Bhai.'

Bhai goes along with the handshake in the spirit of the moment. 'All right, all right,' he says, withdrawing his hand. 'I'm going to excuse myself from the table for a minute.'

'Toilet? asks the man.

'Yes.' Bhai is exasperated. Anyone else would have been dead by now for such impertinence. Mithun comes around the table to join Bhai.

'So you both like, go *everywhere* together?'

Bhai lets it go, simply walks away. He goes into the men's room. That man. He shakes his head. They're different species. Bhai wonders which species would die out first. Probably his. The world would soon be full of Managers. He uncords his pyjamas and pees. His eyes to the wall, hands on his cock. Defenceless. The loo makes a man vulnerable to attack. Any loo he's in, Mithun will be stationed outside.

When they return, the man is facing the other way. He has moved his chair closer to the stage, and is watching Chandni with his mouth open. Bhai is flummoxed. Why is she back on stage again? She finished ten minutes ago.

The man ushers Bhai into a chair next to him, respectfully enough, Bhai notes, and says, 'While you were gone, the men started swearing at the girl on stage, a skinny one who seems to have no experience in dancing, and started yelling for this 'Chandni' to come back. The girl fled in tears.'

Bhai nods, hiding his discomfort with this unexpected collision of his private world with his public. 'Man', says the man, 'she's an angel. I've been to strip clubs in LA and New York, had lap dancers in London and Amsterdam – I could tell you stories about Amsterdam – but this is something else.'

They both watch Chandni in silence for some time. She wears a parrot-green khagra-choli with heavy gold embroidery. Her lips and eyes are made up, her hair twined with flowers. There's henna on her hands and she wears anklets thick as rope. The music is tinny Bollywood crap. Recycled tunes, recycled lyrics, but Chandni makes it all sound like poetry.

She spins and pauses, casts her eyes on the men, her look coy and worshipful of them. Even the meanest prick amongst them is a lord in the way she sees him, conveying, through the movement of limb and eye, the knowledge that she's beautiful and desirable and all his. She never once flaps her khagra up and down. Her legs, breasts and everything about her are full of possibilities. Bhai can see the shape of her, feel her with his mind, but the sum of her lies just beyond his reach.

'Tell me,' says the man, 'how do I get hold of this girl?'

'You can't,' says Bhai

'Is she your babe?' asks the man, startling Bhai into taking his eyes off the stage for a moment.

'Definitely not,' says Bhai with vehemence. He doesn't want the rascal to corrupt his idyll by speculating about it. It is that pure.

'Is she some other gangster's moll then?'

'You think it's my job to know these things? About whom every nautch-girl is connected to by flesh?' Bhai speaks while still focussed on Chandni, who is speeding up as the music goes into its final chorus.

'No, of course, so how can I get in touch with the girl, should I call out to her, or should I go backstage?'

Chandni takes a bow and runs off the stage. Bhai turns once more to the man. 'Let's go back to the table,' he says.

After they're seated, Bhai speaks. 'I don't know how it works with your foreign girls, but here things are different. You cannot, under any circumstance, get in touch with a nautch-girl. If she fancies you, picks you out of the audience, then she will ask for your number and call you. She may or may not demand money from you; that depends on how you behave with her, and how much she likes you.'

That subdues the man. Bhai, on the other hand, is cheered. His Chandni is a queen among all the nautch-girls. How beautiful and how popular. She is good for another two years at least before she retires. Should he wait that long, or should he declare his love for her the very next week?

With difficulty he brings his attention to the man, and the business that lies on the table. They discuss details and legalities for the casino. Then Bhai proposes the casino be named after his father.

'Muthappa Rai Palace,' he announces, and from the corner of his eye, he sees Mithun nod vigorously.

'No way,' says the man. 'It sounds country-bumpkin. No no no. It has to be sexy and city-slick. I have a few options here,' he clicks his briefcase open and rummages out a notepad.

Bhai holds up a hand. In his world, that is the final gesture, the climax of the movie. He says, 'It isn't up for discussion.'

The man thumps his notepad once on the desk. 'Everything can be discussed and a compromise can be reached. Let me see, we could drop the Muthappa and keep the Rai, which is short and stylish. Rai Place. See? Place and Palace, even though the difference between them is only the letter a? Palace is so,' he squirms theatrically on his chair, '*so* so-so. Place is so London. Rai Place, or Rai Palais, even more...' He smacks a kiss on his fingertips. 'It could be any Rai, very popular surname, and nobody will think it's Muthappa Rai, which is a good thing. We don't want that kind of notoriety.'

Sure the world's changing and he must keep up with the times, but how many damn allowances is he supposed to make? Bhai opens his mouth to retort, when a little boy runs to their table and taps on the man's shoulder. The man turns to the boy and Bhai closes his mouth.

'Chandni wants your phone number,' says the boy.

There is a buzz in both Bhai's ears. He pulls an earlobe, but it won't go away. His eyes burn and his mouth is dry. His Chandni. Now the man's. Just like that. He gets up and goes to the toilet again.

Mithun comes in and stands behind him while Bhai stares into the mirror.

'We have his idea,' says Bhai, after a few minutes.

'Yes Bhai.'

'We don't have his government contacts, but the contacts are people, and people are pliable.'

'Yes Bhai.'

'We can get another manager, the city is crawling with them.'

'Yes Bhai.'

'We can even get a woman. I've always wanted a female business partner. Who better than a woman to get men to spend money?

'Yes Bhai.'

'A woman in her forties, with experience and steel, someone in the top of her business, so she'd have dealt with assholes like that man, even assholes like me,' Bhai's mouth curves in the beginning of a smile.

'Yes Bhai,' says Mithun.

'So we don't need him do we?'

'No Bhai.'

'Let us say goodbye to him then,' says Bhai.

My Flirtation with Karoshi

Michael Owen Fisher

Before

I listened on the doorstep. Eventually I shut the door, which had always made the same obtrusive clink no matter how it was closed, and I was convinced Anna's sobbing then became louder. Perhaps I am cynical. Our hallway floor was littered with the glossy hearts we placed on each other's mail and beside our mugs of tea. The only light came from the living room. Filling in the missing information was straightforward, like the situational equivalent of Kanizsa's triangle. I bent down to pick up the vanity box, which still held two of the hearts, and placed it on the table.

I said very little. The only words I remember hearing with any clarity are, 'Why does it always have to be so complicated?' And so I left a woman I still loved in many ways. Staying with my mum for a week helped sidestep the awkwardness of packing toe-to-toe.

Anna sent me a two-line email. The second line said that she had left the DVD player for me. My books were slumped on the shelves like the fallen. Now they were half-emptied, it was clear how bowed the shelves had become. I moved to Golders Green; I had grown up there.

As part of a new routine I started to read Sherlock Holmes on my journeys to and from work. *The Blue Carbuncle*. *The Speckled Band*. Watson and he were the original odd couple. When I realised that for several consecutive evenings I had been unable to focus on any of the words (not simply to *concentrate* on them, but to *see* them in anything resembling a fogless state), Holmes was displaced by *Classic Visual Illusions*. Freemish crates. Penrose stairs. Glossy colour plates of mind-bruisers. After another week, I became too weary to flick through the illusions, even before work. Now I merely close my eyes and look forward to arriving at the office.

The office has become my redoubt. I travel in quiet carriages before and after the bustle of the rush hours. I type, sometimes until my fingers start to turn white. When I go in on Saturdays and Sundays I have an exciting sub rosa sensation. I work every day, every weekend. I grow databases piecemeal. I stare at the screen until I am blunt and my eyes are dry acid. Most of all I look forward to the feeling when everyone else has left the building and I can turn out all the lights except for my desk lamp and stare out over the embers of the city.

At night I fall onto my bed. I cannot remember the last time I used my bathroom mirror or sat in my living room.

My sister, Emma, rang last week to tell me that our mum was worried. 'Look, Benny. *I* know you're fine. You're the coolcat.' Emma had called me this since we were very little. Now she only used it over the phone. 'But mum's worried you're never at home. She tries phoning you Benny. And I think she's been remembering dad quite a bit recently.'

My memories of my father have been pared in the seventeen years since he died. I can see from my photos that he had an impassive, muscular, but gentle face, and inexpressive eyes. But I also remember the tic above the left eyebrow, the quietest of wry smiles and the way his nose would twitch, which I think was more of a mannerism than a tic.

He was born Norihiro Sakagami in Nagoya in 1946, but everyone called him Nori. He immigrated to London in 1970, and a few years later met mum 'at a party.' He always said this as if it was possibly the only party to which he had ever been. He became a father to Benjamin, whom everyone now calls Benny, in 1979. He liked to have chrysanthemums in every room of the house. He died, when I was twelve, in 1991.

Subarachnoidal haemorrhage was written on his death certificate. Although my mum knew that he had worked himself to death. I am unsure what hours he worked, but I remember not seeing him at all during some evenings. One night, as we were returning from the cinema, mum asked Emma and me to stop at dad's workplace to bring him home with us. The building disappeared into the dark sky above us. The atrium was lit peacefully and manned by a receptionist who was at first suspicious, then condescending, but managed to make dad appear eventually.

In Japan killing yourself by working too hard is called 過労死 (*karoshi*). In my early 20s I read about the seven million Japanese who worked 60-hour weeks; the 'idealistic behaviour' of the 24-hour day as a paragon for which workers should aim; the cold management philosophy of *Kaizen*; workers eyeing each other askance. *Gourika-byou* were the diseases of rationalization: spines being wrenched from workers' backs like stubborn taproots. Toilet breaks and sweat-wiping were wastage. I often pictured a frazzled worker collapsing on his sofa, closing his eyes for five minutes, before unpacking his *furoshiki zangyou* (wrapped work) from a brown paper doggie bag.

I have no pressure of this kind. My boss is a ponderous, saggy-faced man who likes to make jokes about homosexuals and women. He told me a few weeks ago to 'go home before that chair gets hungry and eats you,' and occasionally threatens to throw cold water over me unless I leave early.

I considered that I might be paying ghoulish tribute to my dad. Not in a deliberate way, more through the process whereby all sons sop up their father's grubbiest traits eventually and adopt the habits against which they once rebelled. Sometimes I wonder if I am trying to better him, prove I am stronger than him by working these 14-hour days. I have realised, however, that I work to stop myself thinking: to avoid those achingly quiet moments of dolour late at night, when a slight thought can nag and irritate until, like a mote of grit becoming an oyster's pearl, it swells into a sleepless night. In these moments everything feels so insignificant but also very frightening. I think about what I have not done, about life after my mother, about Anna's digital moods and how I miss her arms around me.

During one of these nights I concluded that complicated relationships are an illusion. Things are very simple from each person's own perspective. A complicated relationship is where the perspectives shoot by each other.

Yesterday

I stepped from the office into a rainstorm. 'How similar the raindrops hitting the windows sound to crackling fire,' I thought. I had decided to phone my mum from the office. She had sounded less concerned than I expected, possibly happy.

I opened my umbrella and squinted at the puddles' dark golden reflection of the streetlights. A girl, roughly my age, was sheltering beneath the large tree by my building. She wore a blue halter. Narrow cords and beads of water worked their passage through the boughs and leaves before tumbling to the pavement around her.

'You look like you need it more than me.' I offered her the umbrella. Wearing a suit made me confident that I appeared respectable and less like a late-night creep.

'Oh, thanks,' she responded, looking uncertain. 'But you'll get soaked.'

I waved my hand to reassure her that I would be fine. 'Are you going this way?' I asked.

She nodded. 'Yeah. I was hoping it would be a quick shower. Just stopped for it to pass over.' We started to walk. 'Have you only just finished work?' she chuckled.

I imagined that she was expecting and perhaps hoping for me to say that I had been in the pub for four hours. 'Pulling a late one,' I responded, turning to smile at her through the rain. This was untrue. I had left work later than this twice during the week.

Thunder grumbled overhead. I clasped a hand to my stomach, which caused her to glance at me. 'My dad always told me to protect myself when I hear thunder,' I smiled. She raised an eyebrow, suggesting I needed to expand my explanation. 'Raijin, the Japanese thunder god, enjoys eating bellybuttons.'

She laughed nervously and smacked a hand on her own belly, wearing an expression of mock fear. 'What do you do?' she asked after a few moments.

'Er, I develop headaches. I'm pretty good at cultivating top-of-the-range headaches.' I felt pleased with this mysterious answer. As we approached the underground station I asked her where she was going (a friend's birthday celebrations) and said her dress looked very nice and that I hoped it was staying dry. She thanked me. 'I'm taking the tube so you hang on to that,' I said to her, wiping the runnels from my forehead.

'I can't do that. It's a really nice umbrella.' We looked at each other for a second.

I told her that I didn't know her name, which turned out to be Lisa. 'Benny.' For some reason I shook her hand, which made her giggle. 'Here's my number. Maybe you can give it back to me when the weather's a bit drier.'

Despite the excitement of an unexpected conversation I drifted asleep on the tube as usual.

Today was lost again

The columns of numbers on my monitor were smeared-out and hazy. I could not drink a coffee without feeling sick. It was an effort to even pretend I was typing, or annotating, or reading. I sat at my desk for the afternoon, trying to close my eyes whenever I could, before sneaking away at six thirty. A text message was waiting when I switched on my phone:

Hi Benny, thanks so much for the brolly last night. Hope you stayed dry!

Maybe we could meet for a coffee so I can return it to you. Lisa ☺

I arranged to meet Lisa in *Cups & Chocs* by the river on Saturday. I sighed at myself in the mirror as I searched for a calendar in the box of unpacked odds and sods by my bed. From the box I dredged an old football figurine, years of birthday cards bundled with rubber bands, a poster of Audrey Hepburn, but no calendar. I whispered to myself, out loud, as if somehow it heightened my obedience, 'I'm not going to work this weekend.'

Rip-off

Rachel Bentham

What started it was an old ticket machine in the window of the Sally Army shop. Normally I never went in there because my ex-girlfriend Lou, that I had a lot of respect for, said they traced missing women, which was bad. Maybe not bad if they were runaway teenagers, though even they might have had their reasons, but bad if someone wanted to be missing, like to get away from a violent husband. I'd seen my dad belting my mum when he'd had a few, and I used to wish she'd take us and leave. I left once he put his fists up to me.

So there it was, in the window, sweet as a nut. It had a kind of cartoon face, with two screw heads set apart like two eyes above the straight mouth slot where the ticket came out. When I went in and asked to try it on the old dear looked surprised, but when she saw how it looked on me, she was taken with it too.

'Fits like a glove,' she smiled. 'You really look the part.'

And I did. It was light and comfortable, with a nice wide leather strap that fitted over one shoulder and across my back. In the mirror I looked like Gary Numan on *Top of the Pops*. I stroked the curve of it, like an extra belly. I turned the handle on the side and out slid a ticket with a sound that made my teeth feel sweet.

I tore off the ticket and gave it to the old dear. 'That'll be fifty pence, please.'

'Go on with you,'.she said. Old people like to have a joke; they've got time for it. 'More like five pounds, my love.'

It was three pounds, a bit steep, but it turned out to be the best investment I'd ever make. When I got home I worked out the mechanism – you set the letters and numbers and it printed them. The serrated edge to the mouth slot allowed the printed section to be torn off neatly.

At first I didn't have a plan, I just wanted to try it out. Usually I wore black trousers anyway, and I had a black Harrington jacket from when I'd gone to college in Manchester. Put together, they looked quite official – not exactly a uniform, but smart enough to be taken for some kind of work outfit. What I wanted was to be unnoticeable, official.

It was spring, and sunny, so I thought of the Downs and the way people parked along the bit nearest the Gorge to look at the view. I'd never seen any police or traffic wardens up there. It didn't take long to set the machine with 'Parking: Downs' and the date: 24th March, 1979. It took me longer to decide what to charge. Enough to be believable, but not so much they'd complain or argue. 30p, I decided – you could buy a book for that in those days. I put the ticket machine in a plastic bag. In the bus I held it on my lap. It felt precious.

Clouds were blowing across the sky as I walked over the open sweep of the Downs. I remembered walking there with Lou, how she was taller than me and talked louder than necessary. She'd had brothers to compete with. I'd liked her, but she'd got cross with me for not being ambitious. She'd left me for some muscly bloke just back from Palestine, very right on. Anyway, there weren't many cars about. I felt nervous – I kept fiddling with the bag; what if someone went and got the police? I could say it was for charity, but I knew that wouldn't wash. Just to make sure there was nothing about free parking, I went and read the notice-board near the men's toilet. Labradors and spaniels were being walked by ladies with hairdos that reminded me of Margaret Thatcher. These people could afford thirty pence.

I needed a wee so I went into the toilets. I used a cubicle even though there was no-one else in there; then I got the ticket machine out. Putting it on made me feel serious, excited. Butterflies fluttered in my stomach. About half a dozen cars were parked along the road that curved along the edge of the Downs when I came out. I straightened my back and approached the first one, jangling the change I'd brought. Smile, I told myself, but not too much – try for one of those brief, official smiles that end at the eyes. Turning my head to look out over the Gorge, I practised the smile.

The car was an ugly Austin Maxi. The woman in it was fortyish with brown hair and a sweatshirt. She looked like somebody's mum – what was she doing here? An assignation? Assignations were probably good – she'd want to pay up and send me on my way. In a leisurely fashion, I walked up to her window and bent down. She was smoking a fag so it was open.

'Morning madam. 30p for the parking, please.'

She looked surprised. My heart was going, so I straightened up as if I had all the time in the world, leaning back on my heels the way waiting officials do.

'Oh,' she said. 'Hang on.'

She stuck her cigarette in the corner of her mouth and leaned over to her handbag. I looked along the road; I could always run. Her hand appeared with three 10p coins in the palm. I pocketed the cash, turned the handle and tore off her ticket.

'Thank you.'

She nodded and took a drag on her ciggie. Wow. That easy.

Out of all six cars, only one put up any resistance.

'That's new; charging for parking up here?' He had a posh voice. Some men like to show they know what's what.

'Council policy,' I replied as if I'd said it hundreds of times before. '30p, sir, please,' I repeated, just to remind him what a paltry sum it was. He was sitting in a black Audi with the Financial Times propped against the steering wheel. People who think they're clever question things, but sometimes it just makes them look like arses. Anyway, he paid up.

It was quite a buzz, even for 30p. I stopped and gazed down into the Gorge, watching a gull fly along above the surface of the river. There were thick banks of mud on either side. I wondered what it'd be like to jump right into the silk of them. I turned away. There were plenty more cars further along, by the wooded area where lone men nonchalantly wander off among the trees. Those sitting in their cars would probably cough up smartish, no questions asked.

They did. Morning sir. My official smile was now well practised. When I'd made ten pounds I went and had coffee in

Princess Victoria Street. It was almost too easy, but I could see there were flaws. Approximately every tenth car, someone questioned the charge.

'It used to be free on the Downs.'

'I didn't know there were charges. Why haven't we been informed?'

It would only take a few letters of complaint to the council or the paper for suspicions to be raised. I could keep at it for the afternoon, but it would be too risky to do more than a few days. The tricky customers were the best; it was fun finding new ways to deflate them, developing a nice jobsworth kind of dip at the knees as I responded.

'Oh, I know, sir, you can't get anything for free any more, can you? That's the way the world's going…'

Sympathy was good; who can argue with you if you agree with them? At around four o'clock I decided to call it a day. I'd made just under fifty pounds – not bad at all. As I walked past the zoo, a woman was packing her kids into an estate car near the edge of the parking area. A picnic hamper spilled over the pavement. She was leaning in, organising the kids in the back. I remember thinking she must be one of those perfect mums, taking them to the zoo, picnic and ice creams, everything organised. I stopped and picked up the hamper, handing it to her as she turned round.

'Oh my God!' She was flustered, wide-eyed. Quite attractive in that posh, groomed sort of way, like a pony: bouncy, shiny haired, a lot of teeth in her smile. I still had the ticket machine on. I'd got used to it. 'Should I have paid? I'm so sorry!' She smiled apologetically, shoving the hamper in and grappling with her shoulder bag. 'How much?'

'No problem, madam. I didn't see you earlier; have you been here all day?'

'Sorry – I didn't realise. I wasn't avoiding…'

I nodded, all understanding and calm.

'That'll be one pound then, please.'

As she drove off, I cast a calculating eye over the parking area. It was quiet, maybe only fifty cars or so scattered over the large grassy area in front of the zoo. Most people were leaving. I doubled my day's takings. There was room for a lot more cars. I went home and thought it through, and the next day went and got BCC embroidered on my jacket – Bristol City Council, maybe . . . My name would be Bob. I introduced myself at the Zoo's ticket office once the morning rush was over.

'Hello 'Bob Numan – parking attendant. Nice to meet you. There's been some concern about the levels of crime up here. Apparently there's been a few break-ins; bags left on seats, broken quarter-lights, that kind of thing. I'll be here from now on to keep an eye on things. '

I was careful not to actually claim I was from the council; I was straightforward and workmanlike. The woman in the kiosk liked me, I could tell, but I was careful not to be too friendly.

'I'd better get on, then. But if anyone reports any further problems, refer them to me, alright love?'

After a couple of days I got a camp chair. In the summer I made a sign and sat under the shade of an oak when I wasn't collecting. One pound for cars and five pounds for coaches. Everyone seemed happy, and the vehicles were safe so no one complained. I made three or four hundred pounds most days. When winter came I invested in a wooden hut and a heater. I read books when it was quiet and thought about what I could do with the money. Obviously I couldn't pay tax. The seasons came and went, and sometimes I wondered how long I could go on without getting found out. I lived quietly, putting the cash into different banks then shifting it into investments. After a few years I got a Swiss bank account. Sitting in my hut all winter, I read travel books about Peru, Cuba, Madagascar, Tibet. Sometimes I read the Financial Times.

For almost thirty years I sat there, always polite, keeping myself to myself. I was known for it. Well, I didn't want to give any cause for complaint, did I? It probably made me a different person, living with the knowledge I could be caught. Of course it affected me. I couldn't really have a girlfriend; women ask too many questions. I never got blasé. Close friends would be too risky. My mother got Alzheimers and died in a home. I think she was disappointed I turned out so dull. Every day I changed the date on the ticket machine. After a few years I got an electronic machine that was smaller, lighter – but I missed the beauty of the old one. It was shady, under that tree.

On the news they said I'd made over three million quid by the time I left. The Zoo rang up the council requesting a replacement parking attendant.

'What attendant?' they asked.

A Mountain Fastness

Henry Shukman

The night before all this, Raul David and I got into a long debate about rationality. Me: reason is the basis and extent of human knowledge, therefore what is 'irrational' must be erroneous. Him: the word 'irrational' is a misnomer, for it implies all that's not rationally provable may as well not exist. Whereas there should be a third category, 'ultra-rational,' beyond reason, outside its scope.

We were driving into the Santa Marta mountains of Colombia. I had been seconded to Col-Tel, the national phone company, from Maracaibo, Venezuela (to which I had been contracted by my Edinburgh employers, Technospar) and if I had a base in those days it was the back seat of the large Ford Explorer in which myself, Jorge Carpintero, and Raul David had been known to spend our nights, arguing over whether to leave the engine on for the AC, or crack the windows just enough to let in a little moist air, but not enough to encourage a wholesale invasion of mosquitoes. I've spent much of the last decade working as an engineer in the world's less developed regions.

The track we were following was a riverbed – dry, but unmistakably once the course of a raging torrent. Boulders and pebbles do not make easy passage in the best of lights, but in the yellow beams of our headlights, it was all but impossible to pick our way.

According to Raul, anyway. He was at the wheel and announced that he was going to stop and wait till 'better light', which we all knew meant dawn.

'*Camino feo*,' he muttered as he turned off into a small pasture.

It was an ugly track, but it was also true none of us relished the prospect of stumbling into a Kogi Indian village with our lights blazing at ten at night, when the villagers were high on chicha, coca and ganja, and whatever else they employed to enliven their sod-bound lives.

Our destination was Huascaran, the Kogi's chief village. We were all uneasy about the mission. In fact I had been included not just because of my familiarity with the junction box at the foot of the telecoms aerial we had come to check on, but also because management thought the presence of a woman might be helpful.

We had got off to a late start. While driving through the market in Valledupar, the town at the foot of the mountains, negotiating the shattered pallets, past-it bananas and slinking dogs, we sprang a puncture. Whereupon Raul discovered the jack was bent and nothing but a *ferreteria* could straighten it out. All this before we'd even set off into the mountains. We didn't hit the track out of town until eleven.

The Santa Marta sierra is an odd range. Just ten miles inland from the Caribbean, without foothill or any other preamble, it rises into snow-capped peaks and bleak moors, among whose fastnesses live the enigmatic Kogi. Much as King George's redcoats sought the highland rebels among their misty retreats, so did the forces of an older Colombia seek to subdue these doughty Indians, until a more enlightened era permitted them the autonomy to preserve their ancient customs and beliefs.

Beliefs – the very word that got Raul and me started on our argument. It was the Kogi's beliefs that had caused them – so Raul insisted – not to make use of the telephone aerial that Col-Tel had generously given them a month before.

'Then they should examine their beliefs,' I retorted. 'They might find a telephone is not dangerous.'

We'd known each other only three months, yet we squabbled like an old married couple. We were so good at it, I'd almost have said we enjoyed it.

Another night's camping, then. The three of us had known plenty of those in the lowlands, but not in the mountains. Once we pulled out our tent and gear we found ourselves shivering; our breath billowed in the Jeep lights as we pitched camp. Dark had fallen not an hour before. We were in for a cold night.

Raul and Jorge gathered and built the fire, and yours truly cooked.

'Don't you *mind* working out in the wilds with all those macho men?' – Mama back home in Edinburgh.

Mind? I hate it. I will never understand how intelligent men can be such idiots, and proudly so. Of all my postings over the years, Colombia is the most baffling. You should see the screen-savers back in the office: pornography to a terminal. You could be in the middle of a candle-lit dinner and if a pretty girl walks past the guy will stop talking, watch her go by, growl a lascivious compliment, then turn back to you with a satisfied smile and say, 'Where were we?' And these are guys with MScs and PhDs.

'Mama,' I say. 'I have to go where the work is. What would you have me do? Tell Technospar, "No thank you. I don't fancy sixty grand a year?" You go where they tell you.'

'And how are you ever going to settle down if you keep gallivanting?'

'A, I can hardly be said to be "gallivanting". And B, by "settle down" I presume you mean "provide me with more grand-children".'

I respond testily that not since Jane Austen's day did anyone find a husband by waiting for him to knock at the door. And Mama already has two grand-children anyway, thanks to my elder brother, who has been obliging enough to settle at the foot of Arthur's Seat in good old Blaebury Road, not a mile from home. 'Could the family not use a sprinkling of the exotic?' I try. 'Haven't we Scots always been intrepid travellers?' But she doesn't listen.

Indeed they are contradictory men. Especially Raul. Molly-coddled yet rugged; uncouth yet somehow elegant; macho yet at times gallant; brutish (he too has an X-rated screen-saver) yet philosophical; superstitious yet intelligent.

The other morning in the office he tossed a tea-towel against the back of a chair, and when it happened to loop itself over and hang there, he shouted, 'Ha! It's gonna be a good day after all.'

Raul's English is a hybrid of American, Spanglish and machismo. Which is more or less how he looks too: fierce eyebrows that shine as if bathed in oil; fleshy pale lips, the lips almost of an African; a straight Caucasian nose, then that thick top of jet-black hair. He seems square-built, chunky like many American men; yet lithe too, like an underfed Latino. I discovered once by accident (his bag was open in the back of the vehicle) that his waist is a mere 28 inches.

We are Exploratory Technical Unit 3, Barranquilla District, and we had been wheeled in partly because I'd had some dealings with tribal peoples. I did a special course in cultural anthropology while studying Engineering back in Cambridge, a whim that curiously has shaped my life.

'Tact is everything,' our supervisor impressed on me. 'Col-Tel made a gesture of goodwill but it seems it was rebuffed. We have no wish to inflame the situation. We merely want to check on our junction box, retrieve it if necessary.'

The situation was as follows: Col-Tel had donated a telecom aerial to the Kogi Indians. The Indians had watched the construction (a mere two days' work) and received instruction in the use of the small box-set, all in stony silence. They don't like to talk with foreigners, apparently. As a result, no one was sure they understood how to use the device. Since its installation, Col-Tel had registered only one call from the Kogi Exchange, and it sounded like an angry message. But as it was delivered in Arhuaco, the native tongue, no one knew what they were saying. Since when, not a word. Radio silence. Enter yours truly.

Nominally I am the boss. I'm a systems manager, which means I'm superior to Jorge, a technician, and to Raul, an analyst. We all know that but put it aside. My best authority, anyway, is not seniority but the fact that my figure does not conform to those of the bikini nymphs on their computers, and my dress, in their eyes, is basically a man's: jeans, t-shirt, fleece, that kind of thing.

Once I have finished cooking up the sausages *al diablo*, I am expected to serve each of them first, and to break off from my own grazing the instant either of them signals that he wants more bread, more beans, another spoon of salsa.

I put my foot down after dinner. 'You can't seriously expect me to do the cooking *and* the cleaning,' I said when Jorge pushed his dirty dishes towards me, then lay back on the damp grass, first spreading his anorak under him. But Raul leapt to his defence.

'*Que*?' Raul began. 'Didn't we gather the wood and build the fire for you, drive you up here?'

I keep my head with these boys. 'You did those things for yourselves as much as me.'

There was silence for a moment: just the crackling of the fire, the tinkle of the brook at the edge of our little field.

Then Raul fetched the bottle of aguardiente from the truck, poured himself and Jorge a shot each in the cap, kicked the sole of Jorge's boot and said, 'Come on, Lazy-bones.'

And that was that: confrontation over. Why? Who knows?

That's why Raul intrigues me: he's so contradictory. He seemed to enjoy scrubbing the crockery at the stream, whistling away with a shot of liquor inside him. He has a way of enjoying things, even the washing of dishes.

These mountains are spectacular. I read about them in Geography A-level. They shelve off the tectonic plate to dizzy heights way above your average stratus cloud, a mere twenty miles from the beach at Bocagrande. In class I had imagined glittering slopes of green, dazzling white cols under the Caribbean sun, while far below you'd see slashes of coraline beach and the sea reaching into haze. Not a bit of it. The sierra may be small – fifty miles shoulder to shoulder – but it wraps itself in the mists, rains and snows of a large range. Paramos and screes abound, as well as deep temperate valleys lost in fissures. It is a mysterious place. You could get lost here for weeks or months on end; indeed forever.

A flotilla of clouds moved on after dinner, revealing a three-quarters moon. It illuminated the whole huge valley. Fold upon blue fold receded into the distance, and far away a razor-edged ridge of black leaned against a bright sky. It was a huge landscape.

In some ways Colombia is a modern country. Plenty of well-educated people, roads full of decent cars, and all the new movies arrive at the multiplexes more promptly than in Edinburgh. Yet there are shanty towns too, intransigent poverty, the rule of the gun, and Indians like the Kogi who reside in the late Neolithic.

When Raul came back from doing the dishes, he was a different man. In his hands a stack of utensils gleaming in the firelight, on his face a smile. He announces: 'Do you realise that we are the defeated going back to claim our dead?'

I smiled. 'That's one way of looking at it. Isn't it a little early to predict defeat?'

'You think they're not using the telephone line because they don't know how to?'

'That's what management think.'

He screwed up his face. 'They don't want it. They don't believe in our technology. They don't believe in us.'

Which was how we got onto the subject of beliefs and rationality. 'They know more than we do. They see things we don't.'

'Such as?'

'Such as things only our great men have seen. Like Bach. You know his famous Chaconne?'

Bach no less.

'Life is a chaconne. Bach taught us that.'

'How so?'

'A chaconne is a set of variations over a ground base. Like life. There's a pattern in us. First we struggle to disguise it, then to escape it, then just to accept it – in that order, as the years pass. But we never get away from it. The same pattern. What we are is already encoded in us. In a kind of cipher no one can see, let alone comprehend, until maybe the very last moments. This is the kind of thing the Kogi see. That is why they are not interested in us. We are deceived by the variations. We think they are progress.'

Silence fell. I found myself looking right into those shining black eyes of his, gilded by firelight.

The only map we had was an old hydrographic survey, a colourless scribble of gradients. The next day, with a moment's scrutiny, we determined the hill on which the antenna ought to have been, and it wasn't there. After a day and a half of travelling through that bleak terrain offering not the least sign of humanity, I had been looking forward to a glimpse of a girder mast with a couple of dishes on top, a reminder that these empty mountains were not all there was to life. We paused at the last pass and scanned the hills with binoculars. Something was unmistakably wrong. Either the map had misled us, or management had. We got on the short-wave and went over the coordinates three times.

'It's not there,' I told them.

'*Sí, sí,*' the reply came screeching back. But it wasn't.

There was nothing for it but to continue anyway.

'I'm telling you, they've got rid of it,' Raul kept repeating. 'They never wanted it in the first place.'

We drove along a footpath down into a valley, a beautiful ancient path of bare white earth with rims of turf either side. We must have made a spectacle when we arrived: a big red four-by-four bristling with aerials, emblazoned with the Col-Tel logo, rolling down the final slope into the meadows at the valley bottom. There was a river to ford, and I imagined it must have seemed something like a violation, the rupturing of an imagined barrier, to see that great gleaming vehicle of ours plunge into the stream and come up dripping, its radiator grinning, on the other side.

A number of small figures ran out through a gate in a long stone wall enclosing the village.

I had not seen a Kogi before. Because of their long plaits and white smocks it was a minute before I realized that the figures who had formed into a line ahead of us were men. I also thought it was an effect of being high up in the Jeep that made them seem childishly small, but it wasn't.

We had pulled up on turf smooth as the golf links back home. No sooner had we left the car, wearing the most conciliatory expressions we could muster, than the rain arrived with a crack of thunder. It was probably a god-send. No one was quite sure what to do, either us or them. It quickly became a true Colombian cloudburst. In seconds the white robes of the dozen Kogi turned grey, their faces streamed. I had to fight the urge to get back in the vehicle.

It fell to me, the boss, to initiate things. Curiously, we hadn't discussed what to do at the moment of arrival. I suppose we all wanted to trust to the goodwill of our mission. After all Col-Tel had offered a gift, and we were here to check that all was well with it.

The thought flashed through my mind: I'm glad they're not bearing spears or pop-guns. Then I noticed the crude-looking machetes each wore aslant in his rope-belt, and thought of our gun. We always have one, stashed in the tool-box between lug-wrench and screwdriver. Standard practice out here (God forbid anyone should tell Mama). Somehow the thought of it wasn't reassuring.

The rain drummed on the car's metal roof, probably an unfamiliar sound to them in their world of straw and stone. We stood facing each other in silence. They all looked so slight, as if they weighed nothing, with an alert lightness about them, like a flock of birds that might fly off at any moment.

Finally I said: 'We have come to help with the telephone.'

An older man with a face wrinkled like a walnut said something I didn't catch, and turned back towards the village. The others grunted and waved vaguely. So we followed.

The Kogi say each village is built on a lake and needs to be paved in order not to sink. You could almost believe it as we scurried through the driving spray. It was an extraordinary village. Cobbled throughout. I found that impressive. It reminded me somehow of a Cambridge college, but built with neolithic technology. An oval wall enclosed it, made of big round pebbles balanced on one another so it formed a kind of lattice of rock. If the Flintstones ever made a rood-screen, it would look like that. The houses were stone cylinders topped with thatch, tweaked in the middle to form sprigs of straw. Out of these coiffes rose trickles of smoke. The whole village was extraordinarily clean, in every way: no litter, no clutter, and somehow refreshing, as if people spent a good part of each day tidying it.

They took us to a broad building with a heavy low door. Even I had to stoop. Inside, in the dark, I could just make out that this was the village shop. A counter ran along one side, behind which hung a shelf stacked with unappetizing tins (pilchards from Portugal). We sat down on boards lining the walls, while the Kogi stood, not looking or talking to us, with solemn, gloomy expressions on their faces.

We were scared. I know I was, and Raul and Jorge clearly were, glancing at one another and at me. None of us spoke; as if to talk might be provocative; as if we were all waiting for someone to arrive.

It turned into a long afternoon of waiting in that dingy shop. The longer we were there, the less charmed I was by Kogi architecture, and strangely, the more appealing the idea of a tin of pilchards became.

Raul and Jorge started discussing something in lowered tones.

'No dark plottings, please,' I told them. 'Nor any heroics. What are you thinking?'

'We need to let them know why we're here.'

'They know. This is not the time to push our luck,' I advised.

'What luck?' asked Raul.

'Equipment may be lost but so far no personnel. Looking from management's point of view.'

We must have been there an hour when something happened. I had been thinking the air was thick with unease. But suddenly I saw that on the part of the six little Kogi men in their stiff white dresses, motionless around the walls, there was no unease. Except I didn't see it, I felt it. I don't even know how I knew – the feeling seeped into me. But it was more than a feeling, almost a vision. There we were, nine human beings in all, in that Hobbit house high up in the strange mountain range, with the rain rustling on the roof, and suddenly it was as if I'd never been anywhere else. I hardly know how to put it. I no longer knew who I was. There was just this twilit space on the overcast afternoon with these dark-faced people sheltering from the weather. I had no idea why any of us were here, but needed none. A feeling welled up. Peace. Love. Warmth lapping at the sides of my skull. Wonder pressing in all around until there was no room for thought. I happened to glance at one of the Kogi. He looked up at me, his eyes shining like glass, and smiled. I felt myself spontaneously smile back. It was as if I couldn't separate his smile from my own. I knew in that instant that this was how the Kogi lived, in this very state of timeless joy I was now tasting. How had they managed to communicate it to me? What was it anyway?

Then the spell broke and I dropped back into my own mind, as it were – though with a glow in my midriff and all over my skin.

I looked at Raul and had a curious sense of certainty about him, that he and I knew one another inside out. He nodded at me, and in the afterglow of that transfigured state, he seemed to be confirming that he recognised it too.

Then a new individual came crashing into the room, a non-Kogi, a westerner with a ring of silver hair, a red pate, and a pair of wrinkled, rain-spattered slacks.

'Oh dear, oh dear,' he began in a thick German accent. 'You should not have come. Why have you? I thought I told you people to stay away.'

It turned out he was Herr Fuller, the only missionary the Kogi allowed in their territory, because he alone accepted their condition that he mention not a word of his own God, but received instruction in the ways of theirs. But I learnt all this later.

'They never wanted a telephone. Why you people couldn't consult them before building on Comachel hill. It's the most sacrilegious thing you could have done. Of all places.'

Raul coughed. 'We saw no sign of the antenna coming in.'

'They've pulled it to pieces and thrown it in the ravine where the dead dogs are tossed. I think it's known as hell. In Arhuaco. Don't you understand? They don't want us. They don't like us. It's not even that they don't like us, they don't want to have anything to do with us.'

I heard what he said but I knew he wasn't exactly right.

'We're the younger brothers of mankind, as you may have heard, obsessed with toys and gadgets. What on earth would the Kogi want with a telephone? I am sorry but now you are here they want to be sure you understand. The *mama* is on his way. And some able-bodied men are steering a two-ton truck to the edge of a ravine but you must let them.'

Raul sprang up at this, but the man anxiously waved him down.

Two of the Kogi stepped to the door and put their hands to their machetes.

'They want us to walk home?'

'I'm not sure what they want. But you are on private property, and in a country like this, that means they can do what they like. Oh dear.'

He had this way of sucking in as he spoke. Oh dear, oh dear, all slurped in through his thin lips. Yet in spite of what he said, he seemed excited, with a sparkle in his eyes.

It was clear to me we should just leave.

'Uh huh,' nodded the German. 'If it is possible.'

We never saw the truck again.

Finally the *mama* showed up, jabbing a little rod into his gourd of coca lime, sucking on it then re-powdering it in the gourd. Then he lit up a crumpled Marlboro.

He didn't look at us, and more or less kept his back to us, perhaps fearful we might give him the evil eye, speaking in low phrases to the assembled men. His voice sounded like it was emerging from the back of a cave, deep and resonant. The whole council-meeting, which is what we afterwards learnt was going on, consisted of the man's laconic, intermittent monologue. Then, without reaching any apparent conclusion, he quietly took his leave.

Whereupon, Herr Fuller seized my elbow and said, 'Come on, right now, not a moment to lose,' and ushered the three of us into the late afternoon sunshine, out of the village.

It was all looking beautiful then – the shining stones, the gleaming roofs, the stream sparkling, and the richly forested hills all around. What these people had: a complete world, a world preserved. It struck some chord in me, as if I myself had once lived in a similar village, a similar world.

The padre's cottage was half a mile downstream, the closest they'd allow. They had not only helped him build the place, they had provided him with a *compañera*, a pretty young woman who was silently tripping about the kitchen when we walked in. She fed us, then he put us up on the floor for the night. It was not yet dawn when he bade us God-speed, and we set off.

It was going to be a two-day walk at most. Water wouldn't be a problem, with mountain streams abounding. The padre's girl had baked us two large flat loaves each, and given us a ball of goat's cheese.

It was a wonderful hike. With the moon just about full and the sky clear, we decided to press on right through the night, rather than curl up and shiver for eight hours. Just before dawn the next day we reached the dirt road, and soon after that we ran into the back-up team. They had come looking for us, and would have called out the chopper that afternoon.

Raul and I continued to bicker, but we never discussed those three days among the hills of the Kogi. He asked me to dinner twice, and I said yes both times, but nothing came of it. I wasn't going to get mixed up in any nonsense at work. I went home as planned that Christmas, and my next posting was Sri Lanka.

There, I tried to explore the local beliefs. I submitted to a local brand of head massage, and even went to a crackpot fortune-teller. But I had the sense that whatever the Kogi had shown me, if I wanted to find it again, I was looking in the wrong places. I wasn't even sure it was something you could look for. In the end it became a distraction.

I don't know what happened that afternoon in the mountains but I just couldn't forget it. Had it been a blessing or a curse? In the end I had to start taking pills just to concentrate at work. That helped shut out the memory of it; though not without a troubling sense of dishonesty. But what the heck, I'm in one piece, I've still got my marbles and some things in life will never be answered.

Raul David used to enter my thoughts quite a bit, I suppose because he'd been there too, that day in the Kogi's mountains. I wrote to him. Once I even called him, a year or so later, from Colombo, but the number was dead. I tried the office in Maracaibo but no one had heard of him, or indeed of me. The old crew had all moved on.

Replacing the towers with rainbows

David Gaffney

'When you live here, in Eggborough,' Mr Fuller said, 'you don't even see the towers. It's as if the towers aren't there. They are *not there* to all intents and purposes. I mean they are *there*, but they're not. Not really. I accept that when an outsider sees a house in Eggborough they notice the big fuck-off power plant with ten huge cooling towers in the background. But that's not what Eggborough people see. They see the sky. So what I am asking you to do is to help me to produce a *more accurate* visual representation of how the houses in Eggborough would look if you actually lived here.'

I showed Mr Fuller how you could use the history brush to wipe over the towers and replace them with blue sky.

'Excellent,' Mr Fuller said.

'How about I add something?' I said.

'What were you thinking of?'

'I was thinking of a rainbow.'

Mr Fuller went to the window and looked out. 'I've seen rainbows in Eggborough. So it's possible. It wouldn't be a lie. But doesn't that mean its been raining? No one wants to buy a wet house.'

'You can have a rainbow in a blue sky,' I said, 'look,' and I showed him what I'd done; a soft smudgy arc of colour, shimmering.

I enjoyed replacing the towers with rainbows, but after a few weeks got bored and began to add tiny unicorns as well, hidden in the dappled shadows of lawns and hedges. You could hardly see them, but I knew they were there, and every time I sneaked a unicorn into one of the photos, that house sold quicker than any of the others. I didn't tell Mr Fuller. Magic had no place in the story of his success.

The three Daves

David Gaffney

Fat Dave thought Budapest was shabby-chic. Little Dave thought Paris was shoe-shop-manager-on-a-mid-life crisis. Big Dave didn't want a repeat of Krakow where they had to put on padded clothing and get chased through the woods by attack dogs. So for a laugh, Big Dave suggested they have the stag in Pontefract, where they'd visited the liquorice museum as part of a confectionary campaign. Little Dave said yes right away, and Fat Dave loved the idea. It would be uber-post-post-ironic-out-the-other-side-and-back-into-being-just-ironic.

Shoreditch media spods in sarcastically tilted flat caps sipping mini-Bollingers in the street. There was even a Wimpy so they could eat burgers off a plate with a knife and fork. It was Little Dave's idea to use the stone troughs in the market place, and the president of the National Drinking Fountain and Cattle Trough Association was so impressed that Pontefract's troughs would be returned to their original use he gave his blessing right away.

The night before the stag, the three Daves donned overalls and went into the town to prepare their troughs. Each Dave had a clearly defined role, set out on Fat Dave's spreadsheet. Little Dave was to dig out the soil and flowers and fit the plastic liner, Fat Dave was to operate the wheelbarrow, while Big Dave had to deal with passers by. But Big Dave didn't need to deal with passers by because no-one in Pontefract paid any attention to the three Daves at all.

Come the night of the stag, each Dave sat on a stool next to his trough and began to drink through a long bendy straw. There were no other guests to cater for because the rest of the Shoreditch crowd had decided it would be more ironic not to come.

After an hour, the Daves began to feel cold sitting by their beer-filled troughs. It was quiet too. A few hardy smokers stood outside the nearby pubs looking into the middle distance, but apart from polite nods, they didn't call across to any of the Daves. No Dave rang or texted any of the other Daves to see how he was getting on at his trough because there was a strict no mobile rule on stags and the three Daves followed this to the letter, because stags were about bonding and getting away from the world.

Remaking the moon

David Gaffney

Mason's house had no garden, no walls, no hedges, no borders of any kind, so the local historians who streamed past on their way to the fascinating sluice gates and flooded mine shaft stared through his window at him rudely as if he were a zoo exhibit. At first he glowered and shooed them away, but they never seemed perturbed. They would smile at Mason in that sarcastic way people with an interest in local history have, then saunter off, trailing their fingers along his brickwork. It was as if Mason and his house were public property, like a puppy or pregnant woman.

After many years of this he decided to give the local historians something to stare at. Every Saturday he would set up a little tableaux; one day he would be playing a lute, another day dressed in Mexican wrestling regalia grappling on the floor with a tailor's dummy. Today he was pretending to stuff a badger and there was sawdust and plastic eyes all over the place. She was young for a local historian and from the way she tapped loudly on his window pane it was possible she suspected Mason mights be an automaton operated by the council's heritage curator. She had a mouth that looked as though it was smiling even when it wasn't, and eyes that closed from time to time as if she were in some sort of ecstasy. Mason did something he had never done before.

He went to the front door and opened it.

She wore a green skirt with red tights a yellow jumper and a purple hat. When Mason addressed her she spoke to him in a breathless, hurried voice, closing her eyes in a weird half-asleep way.

'I'm from next door,' she said.

'Oh,' Mason said

'No one stops to look through my window any more. They all come straight to your place, to look at you.'

He paused for a moment to allow this information to settle.

'No one has paused at my window for a long, long time,' she added.

'I see,' Mason said. 'Maybe you should come in.'

Mason made some tea and chopped some fruit and they sat on the sofa together, eating and drinking slowly. When they had finished he took her hand in his and she let him, closing her eyes every now again in that wistful way she had.

'Do you want to do a jigsaw?' Mason said.

'Yes,' she said.

Mason went to his puzzle cupboard, located the Moon one, and tipped the pieces on to the floor. Every piece looked exactly the same. They got down on their knees in the sawdust and plastic eyes and began to assemble it. Local historians looked in on them as they remade the moon. One of them, a round-faced bearded man, caught Mason's eye and winked and the man looked happier than any local historian Mason had ever seen, as if by watching Mason and the young woman remaking the moon, something had been added to him.

How the taste gets in

David Gaffney

Barry's dad didn't have long left so Barry tried to get him whatever he asked for and you never know, maybe Ewan McCall, poet of canal and factory, did play the Longfield Suite in Prestwich and if he did, maybe he did stick a plectrum behind the mirror in the dressing room.

The doors to the Longfield Suite concert room were clothed with heavy curtains and Barry pulled one back to reveal a row of wheeled hospital beds on which lay a group of middle-aged ladies dressed in chiffon, bells, and feathers. Belly dancers. But the ladies weren't belly dancing. Tubes in their arms led to plastic bags filled with dark liquid. He wondered whether this was some secret government experiment, but an examination of the posters in the foyer revealed that a woman called Katy ran a belly dance session every Saturday morning. The blood donor session followed it and the ladies must have agreed to help out.

But who would want belly dancers' blood? A real belly dancer's, possibly, but these women? Middle-class council workers with a hunger for the exotic. His father required a blood transfusion every month, and Barry knew what he would say if he discovered the blood was from a Prestwich belly dancer.

A couple of nurses were laughing with Katy, the red haired dancing instructor, who was demonstrating some moves. Behind a screen sat a large blue box with red tape handles.

That night he sat with his feet up on the box of belly dancer's blood watching Top Gear back to back on Dave and drinking lager. The box wouldn't fit in the fridge so he didn't know what do with it.

In an advert break he picked up his lager and went to the window and looked out at the tomato plants his father had insisted he put in. The brand was Outdoor Girl, so everything fitted, and he took a sachet outside and dribbled it slowly onto the soil.

A couple of months of this treatment gave him the best crop of tomatoes he'd every seen, and when he took one to his father the old man sliced it in two, lifted it to his nose, and inhaled, long and deep.

'That, my son, is a tomato,' he said. 'I want to know everything you did to get it like that. Sit down and tell me,'

Barry sat and spoke to his father for a long time, longer than he'd ever spoken to him over one single period in his life. The fact that it might have been shreds of Ewan McCall's plectrum sprinkled into the feed made his father laugh, and it was nice, because he didn't use to laugh much, at least not when other family members were around.

Come and play in the milky night

David Gaffney

Maureen was involved in everything. She directed the North Cave players version of What Anniversary, she was a regular at American square dancing, she ran the friendship quilters spring coffee morning, booked songstress Bobby Mandrell for the sports and social club, organised the Red Kite lecture, purchased the blue bells for the millennium walk, sourced a special cleaning solution for the war memorial, ran the shoe and handbag sale at the pub, introduced the concept of silent auctions at the WI meetings, and she had become an important mover and shaker on the parish council having been key in getting the woman on Howden road to cut back her bushes. Maureen was woven into the fabric of village life and even though no one knew anything about her, or exactly where she lived, or whether she had any family, we accepted her as one of us.

The letter from East Riding district council thanked North Cave Parish council for its swift response to its query about the number of rough sleepers in the borough, a figure they required so they could report against the government performance indicators. However they were not happy with North Cave Parish Council's answer, which was nil. East Riding Council had information that contradicted this figure. They understood that a person was indeed sleeping rough in the parish of North Cave and the council required this situation to be investigated, and the reasons for the person's homelessness established so that the rough sleeper in question could be helped to access appropriate council services. Winter was approaching and no one should be allowed to sleep rough in cold weather, especially in an area which was, after all, one of the most affluent and pleasant parts of East Riding. An additional problem was that if it was established that there were no rough sleepers at all in the parish of North Cave then part of the council's housing support grant could well be redirected to more so-called needy areas like Hull.

Everyone on the parish council was surprised at the letter. North Cave was not the sort of place where people slept rough. But they agreed it should be investigated and that night Ron Durney, leader of the parish council, went out with a torch and searched every hedge and every bush and every field, every barn, and every outbuilding. He looked behind walls and even up trees. It was a last minute decision to visit the wetlands. The wetlands were well managed and regularly patrolled by the wetlands trust staff, and there were many specimens of scientific interest in the wetlands, including recently, the protected emperor dragonfly. Rough sleepers would be unwelcome.

He was shining his torch at the water's edge, disturbing a group of ducklings with their mother, when he heard foot scrapes and turned to discover Maureen walking along with a rolled up sleeping bag. She was returning from a late meeting with the environmental committee of East Riding Council where, on behalf of the Parish Council, she'd been following up on an enquiry about the North Cave road sweeping rota. She saw Ron Durney's torch beam swish from her face to the rolled up sleeping bag and back again and he shone the torch on himself so she could see who it was.

'You've caught me, Mr Durney. Come with me and I'll tell you all about it.' He followed her to a bench and they sat down.

'Mr Durney, I always wanted to be part of a community like North Cave's. I live in a high rise flat on the outskirts of Hull. I used to visit Howden and North Cave on Sundays with my kids, and I used to read on the village notice-board about all the village activities and I thought how lovely it would be to be part of such a busy, warm community. The kids left home and I thought why not?' She stood up. 'I expect you'll be wanting me to leave.'

'Maureen,' Ron Durney said, 'it's not as simple as that.'

'Well, before you decide,' she said, 'come and see how nice it is where I sleep.' She took his hand and led him down

to a raised palette covered in straw, under a tree by the water's edge. Ron helped her unroll her sleeping bag, and watched her kick off her shoes and wriggle in, and, as it was a chilly night and there were several more issues to discuss, Ron got inside the bag as well. He listened to her talking about the social societies and music clubs and walking associations she was part of, and as he listened he watched the stars grow brighter over the wetlands, heard geese and ducks chuckling and tooting as they settled down to sleep, and felt the warmth of Maureen's head as it rested against his shoulder.

Breaking Taboos

Kachi A. Ozumba

When Kay told his parents the topic of his final-year project, a hush descended over the room, magnifying the chatter from the TV before which the family had gathered to await their favourite sitcom.

His father was seated on his armchair, set aside from the others by the freckled antelope-hide that was draped over it, and upon which nobody, not even their mother, dared to sit. It commanded the best view of the TV without any strain on the neck, and of the aquarium that bubbled with gold and angel fishes beside it. Kay's mother sat in another armchair beside her husband's, knitting a pink shawl for the current occupant of her swollen tummy. Kay was on the three-sitter with his sister while his younger brother was curled up on the rug, his eyes glued to a comic book.

Kay's father reached for the remote control and turned off the television. 'Uju, Obinna,' he called to Kay's siblings, 'excuse us. You can see the programme on the TV upstairs.'

Uju cast a glance at her elder brother that said: *You've come with your trouble again*, and rose from the settee. Obinna unravelled himself from the rug and followed with a sulk on his face.

'Now, Kayobanna, what was it you said?'

The glint in his father's eye made Kay's tongue stick to the roof of his mouth. He waggled it free, swallowed and began: 'I-I said I would be writing on…on human sexuality for my final-year project.'

'That wasn't exactly what you said.'

'Em … yes. But it's still the same… in a broad, generic… you know, conceptual sort of way.'

Kay's father remained silent. Only his eyes, which had narrowed further, showed he was smarting. Any attempt to pin Kay down to exactly what he had said earlier would get him veering off into a hair-splitting analysis of words and concepts – the kind of analysis that often got Kay's father stammering at the end of an argument and wishing Kay were still a boy so he could give him a good hiding. He took a deep breath and bellowed:

'Of all the topics in the world, you pick a taboo and say that's what you want to research on for your final-year project. What happened to writing about…about…' he stalled as he tried to recall something from *Philosophy Made Simple*, a book he had bought and read secretly, driven by his son's quibbling. 'Yes, what happened to writing about Plato, Aristotle, Aquinas and Descartes?'

He pronounced it *Des-car-tes*, as spelt, instead of *Decart*. Kay would have chuckled had he not been too tensed up. 'Dad, I want to work on something new, something challenging.'

'Oh. I forgot you're Socrates. And there's nothing new and challenging enough for you in the works of those lesser philosophers.' He shook his head. 'Is that what three weeks in the UK has done to you? Fill your head with crazy ideas?'

'Dad, please understand. I had some experiences that showed how ignorant I was on the subject. I just want to remedy that.'

'Oh! So, my son, the Bible is no longer enough for you, eh?' Kay's mum said.

Kay bit down on the reply that sprung to his lips.

His father suddenly began to laugh. It was the kind of laugh one would hear in a psychiatric ward. 'I'm sure your interest in this subject is purely academic,' he said, and laughed again.

'Of course, dad, it is.'

'I bet it is. Otherwise I'll kill you myself and report your suicide to the police. Anyway, this is a matter between you and your lecturers. You'll only get into trouble with me if at the end of the day you come home with poor grades as a result of your crazy ideas.' He reached for the remote control and switched on the TV, becoming the usual pragmatist that never belaboured an issue once he had made his point.

Before Kay could exhale and say thanks, his mother began in a strident voice: 'Papa Kay, how can you allow him? No, he should choose another topic, there are many others to choose from.' She noticed that her husband was no longer listening and faced Kay. 'My son, please try and find another topic, please. You can always research on that topic in private, on your own, if you're so bent on it. People will begin to whisper, get other ideas…'

Kay's mother went on and on until his ears became weary from the monotony of her arguments. He felt she was dressing the same words in different attires and having them catwalk before him in the hope that he would fall for them. But his keen eye readily saw through the colourful dresses, down to the dirty underwear. Nevertheless, he assured his mother that he would take her words to heart and her appeals ended.

Three weeks before, Kay had been thinking of writing on some other topic for his final-year project, something to do with truth and the principle of verification. But that changed after his holiday in the UK.

*

Kay left the toilet and walked back to his table in a daze.

'Hey Kay, what's wrong,' Andy asked, setting down his pint of beer.

Kay slumped into his seat. 'Kissing. Two men. I saw two men kissing and…'

Andy cackled. 'Is that why you look like you've seen a ghost? They're born that way, you know, wired that way from the factory…'

'Shhh! Bring your voice down,' Kay whispered, and cast a glance around the pub.

'What the hell for? It's something natural, like being left handed.'

Kay opened his mouth, but his brain drew a blank.

'What's the matter? The cat got your tongue?'

Kay shut his mouth and began to nibble on his lip. He remembered that he had had to nibble on his lip too during his first days in London, after he expressed shock at the advertisements of men seeking men in the newspapers. Pictures of semi-nude hunks who smiled invitingly often accompanied such advertisements. He looked around to see if anyone in the pub had been listening in on their conversation. A heavily built man, three tables to their left, was staring at them while nodding to the beats of George Michael's *Careless Whisper* playing in the background. His head was clean-shaven, and gold rings hung from his earlobes, eyebrow, lower lip and chin.

The man looked away, muttered to his companion and raised his beer to his lips.

Kay cast a glance towards the toilets. He swallowed down the rest of his beer and wiped the foam off his lips. 'Andy, I think we should go now.'

'What? Are you kidding me? It's only ten-thirty. This is supposed to be your last night. We've just started.'

'I'm sorry Andy, but you know the last few days have been hectic. I'll need a good night's sleep before my flight tomorrow.'

'Well, it's your call. If you say so. Just give me a few minutes to finish my beer.'

'Sure,' Kay said. He glanced up at the television mounted on the wall. Something about a husband who assisted the suicide of his terminally ill wife was being shown. It reminded him of his course mate who had chosen to write on euthanasia for her final-year project. She had formulated the title as: 'Euthanasia: Mercy Killing or Killing Mercy?' Kay had told her he could make no meaning out of it and she had retorted that he was thick in the head.

Andy downed the last drop of beer in his glass. 'Sure you still wanna leave?' he asked.

Kay nodded. He took another look towards the toilets as they rose from their seats.

Early the next morning, Kay was aboard his flight to Nigeria. The events of the previous night were still fresh in his mind. Like a ruminant that had found a cosy corner, he sat and chewed over his experiences in the past few weeks: the explicit newspaper adverts, the men locked in passionate embrace in the toilet, the various explanations he had heard. He began to nibble on his lip again.

Prior to his visit to the UK, Kay had encountered such behaviour just once in his life, but then he was only twelve, and had not really grasped what it was all about. It was during his first year in boarding school, a strict mission school for boys where the day was started with prayers in the chapel and ended the same way at night. On one such morning, after the usual prayers and hymn singing, the principal, looking angelic in his white cassock, had called up two senior boys. One of them was very popular among the students. His name was Edward, but he readily answered when students called him Headward because of the large block he carried on his shoulders.

The principal had announced their expulsion from school and said they had allowed themselves to be driven by the devil and his cohorts, Belial and Beelzebub, to commit a foul and immoral act. Then he launched into a sermon about the fate of Sodom and Gomorrah.

Kay's brows had furrowed while the principal spoke. He tried to pick his way to the students' offence through the labyrinth of the reverend's words. The story of Sodom and Gomorrah in the Bible still mystified him; he could not understand why two whole cities had to be razed to the ground just because some men had demanded to 'know' the strange men visiting their town. His only clue to the offence was the principal's use of the words 'immoral act'. He had been in the school long enough to know that the expression 'immoral act' equals 'sexual offence', but he could not make out the particulars. Could they have smuggled girls into the dormitories? Or were they caught touching themselves? It was only when a student beside him wrinkled his face and said: 'Urghhh! It will be smeared all over with faeces,' that he finally understood. His father had quickly changed him to another school when he learned about the event.

A flight stewardess came by and asked if Kay was OK. She looked pretty, pert and professional in her uniform. Kay answered in the affirmative and returned her smile. She walked on and he reached for the in-flight magazine.

Kay dozed off with the magazine on his lap. By the time he awoke, his project was on his mind. He discovered he had been thinking about it in his sleep. An epiphany nudged at his consciousness; a faint stirring, the budding of an idea to write on something new and challenging. By the time the plane touched down at the Murtala Mohammed International Airport Lagos, the epiphany had enveloped and interpenetrated his being.

*

Kay returned to campus with a spring in his step. He met with his friends and course mates in their departmental library. Surrounded by the bound copies of the projects of their predecessors, and the dusty musty volumes of books – from Plato's *Republic* to St. Augustine's *Confessions*, Kant's *Critique of Pure Reason* to Hume's *Treatise on Human Nature* – they discussed their own projects.

Uzo was all set to begin with his work on diarchy as a way out of military coups in Africa. 'It's the kind of arrangement we need in this continent,' he argued. 'Power sharing: a military president working with a civilian prime minister, and not the white-man's model of democracy.' His subject choice was no surprise to anyone. He had always excelled in social and political philosophy, and was the radical secretary general of the Students' Union.

Desola, on the other hand, was now having second thoughts about her project title. 'Someone told me my original title sounded like something lifted from a soft-sell magazine or a roadside pamphlet. I am now thinking of simply titling it: "Euthanasia and the Value of Life". You think it's OK?' Before anyone could answer she clapped her hands and went on, 'Or maybe I should write on abortion instead. Something like...' she paused and brought her eyes together in a squint. 'Yes, "Abortion: The Debate between Life and Choice". I just want to write on one of the current ethical issues.'

She kept smiling at Kay in a way that got Uzo's eyes narrowing. Her leg would occasionally brush against Kay's under the table and when their gazes met, she would smile again conspiratorially.

'I think writing on abortion would suit you better,' Uzo said. 'No doubt you will have plenty of experience to draw on.'

'Maybe. But if insufficient, would you mind my interviewing your sisters?'

Uzo turned red in the face.

'That's OK you two,' Kay cut in before Uzo could reply. 'Pick your bones when you're alone. Let's face what we're here for.' They had parted ways as lovers last semester after Uzo accused her of having an affair. She had not denied it but calmly explained that he too did the same, that the underlying philosophy of their relationship was that of a confederation: weak centre, loose federating units; and that she was more than prepared for them to operate a unitary system once he was ready.

'Euthanasia seems better,' Bayo, another course mate, suggested. 'It is less sensitive.'

'Great. You've just decided it for me. I'll write on abortion then. "Philosophical Perspectives on the Abortion Debate",' she pronounced with a flourish.

'Good for you,' said Bayo. 'Me, I'll be writing on space and time; "A Critical Examination of the Concepts of Space and Time".'

'Space and time?' Kay was taken aback. He could not imagine why anyone would want to write on such an abstraction. Metaphysics was one branch of philosophy he was not keen on. Its endless quibbling about appearance and reality, form and substance, sometimes irritated him. Is this the real world? Are you real or just a shadow of the real you in the real world of ideas? How are you sure you are really in this classroom and not lying in your bed dreaming? Once, their metaphysics lecturer had walked round and round the class repeating the question: 'What is reality?' Kay had felt like walking up to him, saying, 'This is!' and socking him in the mouth. 'What's there to write on about space and time?' he asked. 'Of course, we all know that there is space and there is time.'

'Are you sure?' Bayo asked.

'Oh, don't start,' Kay said. 'Next, you'll be telling me I'm having this conversation in my dream.'

'OK, you, what are you writing on?' Bayo leaned forward, intending to inflict the maximum damage on whatever Kay would say.

Kay inhaled, filling his lungs with the mouldy book smell of the library, 'Homosexuality.'

Bayo was speechless. So was Uzo. Desola's smile froze on her face, and her leg that had been resting against Kay's under the table lifted off.

Bayo regained his voice: 'What kind of a topic is that? Kay, why did you pick such a subject? Are you sure you yourself are not...?'

Uzo shook his head. 'Kay, I think you're going too far this time. You know what some people may begin to think about you. And not just about you, about your friends too.'

Kay launched into an explanation, telling them about his experiences in the UK and why he wanted to write on the subject. His hands drew many arcs in the air as he spoke, and he hardly paused to take a breath. As he rounded off his speech, he felt the warmth of Desola's leg again.

Uzo shook his head, but this time there was something of wonder in the gesture. 'I must say you've got me all excited. I can't wait to see your conclusions. But it won't be easy. Where will you find materials to start you off?'

'Yes, we should allow him to get going right away in search of materials,' Bayo now stared at Kay with squinted, watery eyes, like those of a person gargling with warm salt water. 'We'll be meeting our supervisors tomorrow, so he has only today left. He should get going.'

Kay tried not to brood over the tone he believed he heard in Bayo's voice as he left the library. He made his way to the campus gate and took a bus to the British Council library in a quiet part of the Ibadan town. He had already scoured the university library earlier that morning with little success. Just encyclopaedia write-ups.

It was past noon and the traffic was light. The sun heated up the bare pan of the poorly panel-beaten bus so that it burnt his naked arm whenever the bus shuddered into a pothole and he was thrown against it. By the time he reached his destination, his arm felt raw and his inner vest had soaked through to his blue shirt, creating a dark patch that looked like the map of Africa on his chest.

Kay greeted the library attendant. Her sparkling teeth contrasted well with the ebony complexion of her face when she smiled. But when Kay asked if they had any books on the subject of his research, her face wrinkled up as if he had unfolded a soiled nappy.

'Books on what?' she gasped.

'Sexuality. I mean, human sexuality.' Kay exhaled slowly while the lady took her time to digest what he had said.

Without speaking, she pointed towards a shelf in the library that was stuffed with biology and anatomy textbooks, and kept looking at Kay afterwards with something he felt was midway between suspicion and revulsion. The look remained with him as he left for the United States Information Service library. There, rather than ask the attendant for guidance, he walked the breadth of the hall browsing and searching till he found a few materials. He made copies and hastened back to campus, looking forward to the shelter of his room.

Kay lived in a tiny box room. The width could not take his outstretched hands. On the door, a departmental sticker proclaimed: A PHILOSOPHER LIVES HERE. The door could only open a fraction before it knocked against the two-and-a-half foot spring bed that occupied two-thirds of the room's width. Jammed beside the bed, below a small window, was a little desk with a chair tucked under it. Opposite it was a hip-high cupboard. Suspended above the bed, nailed to the wall, was a hanging rack for his clothes. A wallpaper of rainbow-coloured flowers adorned the walls.

Yet, on a campus short of student accommodation, where as many as eight students sometimes occupied rooms originally designed for two, Kay's room had the status of a Mayfair or Beverly Hills flat. He had paid a whopping six thousand naira for it, and always accused Uzo of envy whenever he referred to it as a toilet anteroom because its door was adjacent to that of the smelly common toilet.

Kay placed the materials from the library on his desk and sat down. He had to prepare to present his topic to his supervisor the following morning. The list on their departmental notice board showed he had been assigned to

Dr. Mrs. Adenike, the only woman in the department, as his supervisor. He bemoaned his luck. He would have found it easier, felt freer, discussing the subject with a man.

He set to work, tracing the debate on the topic to earlier times, discovering that philosophers such as Imanuel Kant and Jeremy Bentham had taken opposing sides on the issue. From the present day, he had the arguments of Michael Ruse, a professor of philosophy at Guelph University Canada, in the secular humanists' Free Inquiry magazine before him. The categorical smugness with which the professor stated his position on the matter incited in Kay the lust to punch holes in his arguments. He had just started to hum to himself when a knock sounded on the door.

Desola flew into his arms when he opened the door. 'You're a bad, bad boy,' she said through rosy pouted lips. 'You sneaked back into campus without letting me know.'

Alarm bells rang somewhere in the background in Kay's head. He returned her hug with stiff arms. The tight spaghetti-strapped top she wore over a dark mini skirt, felt damp against his arms. Her hair tickled his nose and filled his lungs with the fruity scent of relaxer and the alluring fragrance of her deodorant, which had held on courageously against the sweaty March heat.

'Naughty, naughty boy,' she repeated, still holding onto him.

Kay extricated himself. 'Welcome to my abode,' he said, and ushered her into the room. He reached to position the chair for her. But she sat on the spring bed, kicked off her shoes and began bouncing up and down.

The bells increased in decibel, warning Kay off from joining her on the bed. It was still too early to get involved with her. It would not sit well with his friend, Uzo. *But she'll think something is wrong with you*, another side of him protested as he sat on the chair.

'Strong bed,' Desola said, and bounced with more gusto.

The spring squeaked like a hundred mice. It reminded Kay of the last visit of Gina, his girlfriend who had graduated last session. Like many other campus relationships, they had operated a confederation.

'Nice place you have here, nothing like some privacy. You know, I do not usually visit guys who live alone unaccompanied. But in your case,' she shrugged, 'you may well be a eunuch, a monk.'

Kay shifted on his seat.

'Even your room looks like a Hare Krishna grotto,' she added, looking over the gaudy wallpaper.

Kay's lips stretched wider in what he thought was the kind of all-forgiving smile a pious old priest would give a suggestive member of his congregation. It made him feel like a fox smiling benignly at a chicken. Or was she trying to use him to get at her ex? To get Uzo jealous? He became angry at the thought. He took a deep breath and rose from his seat, 'You know, I've had nothing since breakfast. Come, join me, let me buy you lunch. We can talk while we eat.'

Desola stared up at Kay. Disbelief had formed wrinkles around her eyes. She hesitated for a few seconds, smiled, then began to slip her feet back into her shoes.

'Did you succeed in getting some materials for your project?' she asked as she got up from the bed.

'I managed to gather a few, nothing heavy-duty though, just some journals.'

'So you're now ready for your supervisor?'

'Well, yes. In fact, I was working on it before you came.'

'You and your strange topic. You know, I'm sure your supervisor will think you are…queer.'

Kay turned and looked at her. Her eyes said: *I sure am beginning to think you are queer!*

He smiled. 'Then I'll tell her she's committing the *ad hominem* fallacy,' he said, and shut the door behind them.

The next morning Kay met his supervisor. She was sitting behind a wide desk in a room that looked more like a used books store than an office. When she asked for his research topic, he placed a sheet of paper before her.

The woman lowered her gaze to the paper and Kay saw her eyes widen. A muscle began to twitch in her face, beneath her left eye. When she raised her head, Kay was relieved that she did not give him the soiled nappy look.

'W-why this subject?' she asked.

Kay launched into his arguments, placing his few materials, Kant, Bentham and Ruse, before her to show that philosophers had concerned themselves with the subject over history.

There was a knock at the door.

'Come in.'

Kay turned to see an attractive lady in brilliant white designer T-shirt and black jeans.

'Ah, Ada, come on in,' said Dr Adenike.

Ada stepped in and slid into a chair by the door.

Kay's supervisor continued to talk across the room. 'Ada, this young man has proposed a research topic that has never in all my 25 years of academe been submitted to me. Homosexuality'.

The high-tension pause that followed was now becoming routine for Kay.

'But how can you…' Ada started.

Dr Adenike cut in: 'Ada, I am an academic, trained to assess arguments and check that conclusions are valid. My own emotions and feelings are quite another matter.' She beamed a smile over Kay's right shoulder.

Kay did not need to look round to know that it was being reciprocated.

Dr Adenike handed Kay the sheet of paper. 'I very much look forward to receiving your work. Good luck.'

Teeth

Krishan Coupland

1. *The Kitchen*

There was the time Steve stole about a thousand paper plates from this warehouse he worked at. You don't have to wash paper plates, so of course me and Devon and Steve all started eating off them. We filled up a couple of bin bags with the things, and when we ran out of bin bags we started dumping them in the sink.

That was where it all went wrong.

The paper rotted, sludged down, blocked up the pipes. Water got stuck in the sink, turned yellow and stagnant. Next thing we know the kitchen's full of these little, round, bright-red insects. I went in one night, for a glass of water, and all I could feel were these things batting against my face like moths against a light bulb. Against my eyelids. Against my lips and nose and ears.

So Steve brought home a bug bomb: this shiny black canister about the size of a grenade. We set it off in the kitchen, shut the door and waited. Steve started getting all worried.

'I saw this episode of CSI, yeah?' He scratched his neck and licked his fingernails. 'This woman, she gassed herself to death with one of those things. It got into her air-con.' He said how the woman was all blue when they found her; face and everything.

We didn't have air con, but Steve figured we ought to be safe. We got some duct tape and went all around the door to the kitchen, sealing it off like how they quarantine infectious diseases.

The thing is though, we never un-taped it. None of us ever went back in. It's been six weeks now and sometimes I put my ear to the door and I hear this sound, you know, this terrible, whispering sound.

2. The Cat

'It looks like Hitler.' Devon tipped it out of his briefcase. Its fur was all matted in that gooey stuff the burger place use instead of cheese. There was a neat stripe of black fur underneath the nose. It crouched and mewled and mewled, a small kitten mouth full of black and pink. 'Found it in the bins,' said Devon. 'Just yelping and trying to climb out.'

We weren't allowed pets, but it wasn't like anyone would know. The art students upstairs never came down anymore; they just slipped angry letters underneath our door. The landlord had been missing for weeks.

'It'll keep down the mice,' said Devon. 'Cats do that, yeah? They feed themselves. Better than a dog.'

Steve tried to stroke it and his hand came away all covered in blood and cheese and drowned grey snags of fur. The thing made this noise like a bullfrog.

Steve said, 'I think I might be allergic.' We ignored him; Steve thinks he might be allergic to everything. Devon went and got a bit of dental floss from the bin and dragged it along the floor. The cat watched it, but didn't move.

'Come on,' said Devon. 'Come on.'

I said, 'We ought to wash it. Get all that shit out of its fur.'

Devon snorted. 'Cats wash themselves.'

Just then it made a noise like a baby coughing. We all watched it. It coughed a couple more times, awkward, twisting its head around like it was choking to death. Then its whole thin body shuddered, and something tangled and furry and shining came dribbling out of its pink-black mouth.

3. The White Van

There was the time Steve called me up at work. He'd been fired not long after stealing the bug bomb. He was at home. I don't know how he got my number, but he called me. 'It's an emergency,' he said, the moment I answered. Before I could even ask, he hung up.

So of course, I signed out early and bussed it home. All the while thinking that, like, the house had burned down, or our stuff had been burgled, or whatever. But when I got in it was just Steve, sitting there on the bottom step, unshaved and in his dressing gown, staring.

'The white van,' he said. 'Right outside. It's been there all morning.'

'Yeah?'

'It's one of them enforcement vans. You know, with the people inside? Like spies use. It's been there all morning. Right outside.'

'You said it was an emergency.'

Steve went all small inside his gown. I could smell something. It might have been him; he didn't look much like he'd showered. 'They're right outside, man. They know we're in here. They got cameras and everything. I saw it. On TV.'

'Fucking hell, Steve.' Any other time I would have just gone mental on him. They were cutting back at work and I'd just signed out early for the third day in two weeks. For this. For nothing. I would have yelled or hit him or something, if it weren't for his mum. See, she'd died in hospital last month. You can't yell at someone when they've just had their mum die.

Instead, I took him into the front room and we sat and waited 'til the van drove away.

4. *Boxes*

A few months after the van I lost my job as well. That meant Devon was the only one still working. He made Steve do him sandwiches every morning. I had to iron his shirt and clean his shoes. Devon's always been like that, all smart and bossy and generally a prick.

'I spat in his lunch,' Steve told me, one time, right after Devon had left for work.

'For real?'

Steve shrugged, shook his head. 'No. It'd be good though, man if I did.'

During the day we watched a lot of TV, played a lot of Playstation. We spent an afternoon pouring salt and pellets and stuff on all the slugs in the bathroom. It was cool. There was this one day where we decided it would also be cool to have a look round Devon's room. Normally he doesn't let us in there, keeps his door locked the whole time. We figured he must have something to hide.

Steve went round to the back garden, climbed up on top of the bins and opened the window with a coat hanger. He let me in.

Devon's room is basically the same as mine or Steve's. Clothes and plates and stuff all over the floor. The damp on the walls, all jagged lines like veins. Cigarette-coloured plaster. But there were also these boxes stacked up in a corner. They looked out of place, somehow. Sort of new and important.

So we opened one, me and Steve. We looked inside. Saw the leaflets, weighed in bundles, crammed with words and greyscale pictures. And the words on the leaflets. Wrong words, hate words, and those crazed crooked little symbols. All lined up like rows of teeth.

5. The Art Students

There was the time I passed out in the hallway and the art students brought me in. They must have got my keys out of my pocket. I had been drinking. I don't remember. This was way back, before the white van, before Steve lost his job. He'd been bringing home crates of no-brand beer every other night. Four boxes to a crate. Twelve tins to a box. I must have gone out for some food, and then I woke up to them carrying me inside. Hands under my armpits and my knees. I couldn't move.

One of them was saying, 'Is that vomit? God, he puked himself.'

'Where do we put him?'

'Sofa.' They dumped me down on the sofa. Didn't bother to clear it first. A forgotten spoon dug into my side. Something under my neck split and oozed.

'God,' said the first one. 'How do they *live* here?'

'Fucking pigs. They've got a cat in here somewhere. I hear it at night. Mewling. Probably don't even feed it.'

'God.'

I couldn't see much. Tall, dark shapes moving around somewhere above me. Crunching noises as they trod on beer cans and polystyrene trays. One of them moved over to where the coffee table is. Glass clinked against glass.

'Ugh,' she said. It sounded like she was showing something to the other one. Something she'd picked up off the table. Then, 'Hey. Watch this.'

A second later something cold and slimy spattered against my face. I shut my eyes. Smell of vinegar. The stuff, whatever it was, dripped wetly down my chin, my collarbone, an icy slither underneath my shirt. Something solid and greasy and thick plopped against my forehead and glued itself there.

The art students laughed.

6. *Trouble*

Steve was the one who found it, curled up in a ball underneath his bed. I'd smelled something sour days ago: a vomity smell. But I was used to odd smells in the flat. Didn't think to look. Didn't think how I hadn't had the cat mewling round my ankles for days now. Weeks.

'We have to move it,' said Steve. 'You have to move it. Throw it out.'

I argued, of course, but no way was Steve touching a dead thing. It was down to me. Only, when I went to pick it up something bright white came tumbling out of its ear. A maggot. A fucking maggot. The bottom of the cat's neck was wet with the things, wriggling, blind, pushing out through layers of fur and meat.

Steve made this noise like he was about to throw up. He gulped. 'We're fucked, man. We're fucked. Devon's going to kill us. Oh . . .' He heaved, swallowed, squeezed his eyes tight shut. 'We're fucked, we're fucked, we're fucked.'

I thought of the boxes. We had maybe half an hour before Devon got home.

I got a bin liner and draped it over the cat and scooped all of it up, cat and maggots and everything. It was a soft and hollow bundle. Cold.

All the way through the flat Steve danced around, telling me don't drop it, don't drop it and then I was in the hallway and just about to tell him to shut his mouth when I heard the key in the door. Devon's key. *Devon.* There I was with the rotting body of his cat. It shouldn't have scared me, not really, but there was this slimy feeling in my gut and the memory of what I saw in those boxes and the way Devon goes all quiet and spitting when he's mad.

Steve was at the door and he'd shot the deadbolt and Devon was slapping flat-fisted from outside, calling, 'Guys? Hey, guys, let me in. It's me. Let me in, I can hear you.' Steve put his hands over his ears. I couldn't move. Devon started kicking the door, yelling, 'This isn't funny, let me in. I swear to God, guys. I can fucking hear you,' and Steve doubled over, hands on knees, face pulled back like it was stretched by hooks. His breathing was wrong, too fast, like an asthma attack, like a drowning man, like he was going to die, right there on a bed of junk mail and newspaper and tiles smeared with mould.

A Milking Lesson

Philippa de Burlet

County Cork, 1972

'Wanted to purchase: House with land. Anything considered.'

Jeremiah told us he'd read the advertisement we'd placed in *Exchange and Mart*, laid the paper down, gone about his day's work and then, after talking to May, decided to draft a response. His brother's house, just a short way across the valley, was empty. Jeremiah didn't want to add another derelict house to a landscape echoing with abandonment.

I looked across the table at my friends, hairy and scruffy and smelling of garlic. It was remarkable how welcoming May and Jeremiah were.

Perhaps Jeremiah read my thoughts. 'When ye first came to look at the house I was a bit surprised. But when ye said ye'd prefer yer tea in the kitchen I began to think we might get along.'

'And I said, welcome to Ireland,' and you smiled and showed yer beautiful teeth,' said May.

And that's how it had been when we first met. And then, after May and Jeremiah had fed us, the first of many teas we would have with them, we'd all walked along the lane to the empty house. We'd shaken hands then and there and, the following day, both parties engaged solicitors.

Mr Riordan, who handled the house sale on our behalf, had struggled to find a category for his new clients. 'What profession do ye have?' he asked.

'None so far,' we replied, but the man among us said he'd done a bit of language teaching.

'Are ye married?' was the next question to which we all replied no.

When the sale was completed, Mr Riordan took up his fountain pen and wrote 'Spinster, Spinster, Spinster & Linguist', in a flowing copperplate hand, on the house deeds. Not one of us was older than eighteen. We had a crazy idea about sustainable living (back then it was called self-sufficiency) and had worked to save money. Enough between us, as it turned out, to buy the house and a few acres. There was a lot that delighted us about our newly adopted home. We were, for example, amused that the country was run by someone called 'The Tea Sock'. At school we'd learned a bit about the potato famine and we'd heard the phrase 'Black and Tans' but had no idea what it meant. Much later on Jeremiah told us he'd once been held by four Black and Tans who'd dunked him in the pond looking for some missing weapons. He'd played the part of a stupid, simple boy, one who wouldn't be trusted with a secret, and eventually they'd dumped him in the pond and left. He'd learned to swim that day.

Jeremiah didn't blame us for our ignorance. How many eighteen-year-olds were interested in history or politics, he said. Although when he was our age or thereabouts, he wasn't exactly sure which year he'd been born but he thought five or six years after the turn of the century, things were different. He'd been a lad during the Easter Uprising and the executions that followed; a young man when Independence finally came. He'd been interested in politics alright. He never had a choice.

From the beginning Jeremiah would walk down the lane or across the fields to see how we were getting on with this or that and he'd pass on May's invitation to go over for a bit of tea. And any time we needed to know something about cutting hay, killing a pig or what size timber to use for rafters, we'd walk up the lane to ask May and Jeremiah.

One day, as I approached the house I heard Jeremiah's voice through the open window. 'D'ye think one of the girls and the boy could be together?'

'No. Not yet anyhow,' May replied after a pause.

'What are they doing here? They have an education, why aren't they in England at college, or in employment?'

May was inclined to talk with us girls and she was building up a picture. 'I'd say they've made a new sort of family with each other... for the time being. Maybe their own families aren't so close like.'

'Why do the girls dress like boys? Are they...?'

'No, Jerry, they're not.'

'It's their business, but those girls are pretty enough... good and strong too.'

'Jeremiah! Even if they were twice as old there's no man in this parish young enough fer them.'

'Well, that's true. Anyways they don't go to Mass.'

May sighed, and I expect she crossed herself. 'Their garden's looking grand. I niver thought they'd dig the whole field. And 'tis hard to dig and plant and hoe in a skirt,' she said.

'I hear they're going to cut turf for their fire soon. And the roof is goin' ter come off ter make way fer a new one.'

''Tis good to see Connor's old place havin' some care.'

I approached the house whistling to make my presence known.

The back wall of their kitchen was adorned with two pictures; Jesus with his chest exposed to show The Sacred Heart and a black and white photograph of John F. Kennedy. Jesus was illuminated by a small red light set below the frame. Jeremiah didn't care much for either picture but May liked to observe the proprieties. The walls were painted with pale green distemper — May said green was a restful colour — and the room contained a solid fuel Stanley range, a sink with cold running water and, on a high shelf, a small television.

I sat at the formica-topped table with Jeremiah. May, clad in her faded floral pinny which only came off when she went to Mass, was boiling a pan of eggs. The table was set with teacups, small plates and a round loaf of soda bread.

'We've been thinking about yer request,' Jeremiah said.

'Yes?'

'May and I have talked it over and we will sell ye a cow.'

'A grand little heifer we have. Ye'll have to learn to milk and ye have to milk plucky', said May. 'Every day ye will come up here and milk the cows with us and when we say ye are good enough ye can take yer own cow home. You know when she's yer own there'll be a deal of milk?'

'We're planning to make cheese.'

'When Jerry and I were younger we used t' have thick milk in times we didn't have enough food.'

'Thick milk?'

'When it's soured in the pail and the curd has risen.'

'Can I see her?'

'After tea. Now tell us what you think about the election.'

Jeremiah had offered to drive us to the polling station in his black Morris Minor, just as long as we voted in accordance with him.

'How have ye decided to vote?'

'We think Fine Gael talk some sense.'

Jeremiah snorted. 'I hope ye are pulling my leg! I was there when Fianna Fáil was founded and I've voted for them ever since 1932 when they first came to power. Was that the year we were married May? I shan't be wearing out me tyres if youse all vote for them socialists.'

Next morning early I walked across for my first lesson. Small brown hills rose out of stony little fields and bogs lay in the valley floors. When I arrived, Jeremiah issued me with a glass of what he called punch – a measure of poteen, three heaped teaspoons of white sugar and half a glass of boiling water. It was somewhere between cough mixture and paraffin and was dispensed as a treat. I wished I'd had breakfast first.

May, with a collection of kettles boiling on the cooker, was enveloped in steam. She emerged from the mist like a genie and handed me a pair of galvanised buckets.

'They need t'be scoured and scalded and then we'll go out to the cows.'

As we walked across the fields, Jeremiah began to sing. He had a good, clear tenor voice.

> *In 1803 we sailed out to sea*
> *Out from the sweet town of Derry*
> *For Australia bound if we didn't all drown*
> *And the marks of our fetters we carried*
> *In our rusty iron chains we sighed for our weans*
> *Our good women we left in sorrow*
> *As the mainsails unfurled, our curses we hurled*
> *On the English, and thoughts of tomorrow*
>
> *Oh – Oh I wish I was back home in Derry...*

Every time we three spinsters and the linguist went into a bar, someone would start up. It wasn't hostile, but they wanted us to know how it used to be.

Jeremiah carried a stick but it was more for punctuation and poking things than to lean on. I'd seen him vault a gate like he was thirty not seventy-something. He'd never tell us his exact age, just that he was a lad during 'The Troubles'. May bobbed along pretty well too. She reminded me of a robin.

'Our' cow was a beauty, part Friesian and part Shorthorn. Her coat was thick and springy and was a soft blue-grey colour with patches of cream. Her eyes were dark and long-lashed. I was not yet to be allowed to milk her. She was not for beginners. I was to learn on another, older, animal.

The milking house was a small stone barn with a dozen stalls, six down each side, and a rough concrete channel in the middle with straw scattered on the floor. May tipped out a bit of mash for each of the cows as they ambled in, followed by Jeremiah. She hummed to them as we closed the wooden stalls around their necks.

She sat on a stool beside the cow, a two-gallon pail gripped between her knees. 'Ye always milk the two front quarters together and the two back ones together. Ye never go on the diagonal or the same side.' She passed me a warm wet rag. 'Washing the udder encourages the cow to let down her milk.'

'May?'

'What?'

'Tell me about Site of Ambush at Kilmichael.'

'Jerry'd tell ye better.'

Our house was less than two miles from a monument which commemorated in stone a 'Glorious Victory for the IRA' against the British. Oddly, given that the entire parish was keen to educate us about Ireland's struggle for independence, no-one had a lot to say about Kilmichael Ambush.

'Watch,' she said. 'Ye don't ever pull the teats else you'll get a good kicking. Look. Ye use yer thumb and first finger to close off the teat at the top, so the milk don't go back up. Then ye use t'other fingers all together like a press so the milk comes out wi' a good pressure. Ye must keep yer nails short.'

Twin streams of milk hissed from the teats and pinged into the bucket.

'You do it like a rhythm, left then right then left…' The milk frothed into the bucket. 'Now it's your turn.'

I tried to copy what May had done. I squeezed the teats. A couple of drops came out. The bucket felt huge between my knees. 'How much milk will she give?'

'At least that bucketful. Maybe more. Ye have to learn how to milk fast and ye always have t' milk a cow dry else she could get mastitis.'

I tried again for a minute or two and managed to get a few dribbles.

'Lean into the cow more,' instructed May. 'Lean yer shoulder up agi'nst her.'

I moved in closer. I could hear the mighty ruminant digestive system sloshing and rumbling close to my ear. The teats were wet with milk and my hand slipped. The cow kicked in protest at my technique and she caught the side of the bucket. The milk spilled across the shed floor. May handed me back the empty bucket.

'Persevere,' she said and went to milk another one.

Jeremiah gave my cow another scoop of feed and she munched, slurping and grinding her teeth. 'It was November 28th 1920. At dusk,' he said, coming to stand by my side.

I managed three respectable squirts into my bucket.

'Ye've heard of the Black and Tans. They were non-commissioned men serving as military police. A right rabble they were too.' Jeremiah spat into the straw on the shed floor. 'But stationed at Macroom were some Auxiliaries. These were supposed to be an officer class like, an *elite* fighting force for the Black and Tans.'

My bucket now contained about quarter of an inch of liquid.

'Well trained men but we hated them too. They were never shy of burning down our houses, beating and killing and the like.'

May came and emptied my bucket for me and gave me a nod.

'The Auxiliaries had been raiding villages around here. 'Twas very bad. We needed to fight back. The Irish Republican Army, led by Tom Barry, hid in them small hills and waited for the Auxiliaries. They were in two lorries, nine men in each. They was all killed in the first lorry, all shot. It came into position, Barry threw a grenade right in the cab and we opened fire.'

I leaned against the cow. She was warm and solid.

'The second lorry heard the commotion of course and there was a fierce fight. All but two of the Auxiliaries were killed. Tom was twenty-three and he had the command of thirty-six IRA volunteers. 'Twas the first real engagement fer the West Cork IRA and by God we needed it.'

'So why isn't it talked about so much?' I asked.

'It's that the *accounts* of the ambush are different.'

'How do you mean?'

'The British claimed they tried to surrender and our man Barry ordered his men to keep firing. And it was said the last few were bludgeoned and stabbed t'death with bayonets. An' it was claimed the bodies was mutilated with axes.'

My forearms had a burning ache from wrist to elbow and I was sweating. 'How old were you then?' I asked.

'Maybe sixteen or seventeen.'

'And what really happened?'

'There was no mutilation of the bodies but one of the survivors was killed later.'

'And the surrender thing?'

'Well, the last few men showed they would surrender and the IRA stopped firing an' then a shot was fired by an Auxiliary. Well... Barry gave the order to fire and not to stop 'til 'twas all over.'

'And what happened after?'

'After the ambush, the British made reprisals. They were reelin' from the outcome, niver thought we'd fight back like. I could show you a fair few ruins close to here where houses were burned. We had martial law in Cork, Kerry and Tipperary and Limerick. The middle of Cork City was burned the following month. There was terrible violence.'

May carried on milking but the milk wasn't fizzing into the bucket with such energy. It was as though she was holding her breath. I said nothing.

'One thing I know fer sure. 'Twas only the taking up of arms which brought the British to the negotiating table.'

I heard May breathe out. She stood up with a full pail of milk.

'Now we have ter strain it. And how did ye like yer first milking lesson?

I stroked the bony old cow and replied that I had liked it very much.

May was busy with the milk so I let the cows out of their stalls and Jeremiah followed them out. As he walked off swinging his stick he began singing again.

Come all ye young rebels, and list while I sing,
For the love of one's country is a terrible thing.
It banishes fear with the speed of a flame,
And it makes us all part of the patriot game.

My name is O'Hanlon, and I've just turned sixteen.
My home is in Monaghan, and where I was weaned
I learned all my life cruel England's to blame,
So now I am part of the patriot game.

May handed me a container of milk. 'Take it home. Yer fine fer a novice.'

'Shall I come the same time tomorrow?'

'You will.'

The Conservator

Anna Lunk

Late summer, wet, windy, the barometer swings further left than she's ever seen it. She listens to the radio as she works; stitching, unpicking, dying threads; the great hunting scene rolled out before her. There's a strange coming and going between the world of the tapestry and the world of the radio; the huntsmen caught in the woodland clearing seem more real than the political debates, book reviews and consumer advice programmes. There's some news of flooding in the West Midlands, the River Severn bursting its banks and, the bad weather's moving south. Chances are the road between her house and the village will be impassable, the estuary waters swelled by rain draining down from the moors, the wind pushing the tide up river. The car can stay in the garage until the barometer swings back. The food she has left from last week's shop will have to last. On dry days she'd walk the footpaths to the village shop, but there's too much mud with all this rain. Besides she's working to a deadline and it's no bad thing the weather is confining her to the studio. She's checked her inbox for work messages, leaving emails from friends and relatives unopened.

The whirr of the dehumidifier, rain on the velux, the chat of the radio, the feel of the five hundred year old wools and silks beneath her fingers and her own quiet stitching, contribute to an ache in her shoulders. She's started working on a young woman's face. Eleanor, she likes to give them names, stands under an oak watching the passing riders and their sleek dogs. Does she see the stag, his antlers just visible above the thicket of bushes? Is she hoping he'll escape the sharp arrows, the dog's bared teeth, or does she thrill to the chase, the letting of blood? Eleanor's nose is long, her mouth full, though before the initial washing it was barely visible. The colours now sing clear. Her job is to reveal that which centuries of dirt and neglect have concealed and to prevent further deterioration. Nothing should be added, but she can't resist taking up a darker thread; adding a little groove between lips and chin. She repeatedly glances at the photographs of the whole tapestry to enable her to work on the detail. It's easy to lose herself in Eleanor's gaze and disregard the woman on the horse on the far right, currently wound into the roller.

The one o' clock headlines list floods in Tewkesbury and the danger of breached defences along the East Coast. Closer to home a man has been swept off the seafront in Teignmouth. Lady Munro is missing. She was last seen by her housekeeper walking down through the rose garden towards the lake on Tuesday evening. It was raining. Eleanor Munro was carrying an umbrella. Perhaps she mishears the name. But it's the Trustees of the Munro estate who've commissioned this work and she remembers the lake. Lord and Lady Munro were away when she collected the tapestry. Tea was served on the terrace.

'Once you've finished indoors do feel free to explore. There's some good walks down round the lake. It was enlarged in the eighteenth century, but there's always been water there.' It was a blue skied day, a world removed from the dark rain-lashed present. But she hadn't enjoyed the lake. The banks were gloomy with overgrown shrubs and conifers; the water didn't reflect the shimmering sunlight, but seemed instead to mirror darkness.

She glances at the skylights as rain continues to hammer on the glass. And when she looks back there's a tear on Eleanor's cheek. The window must be leaking water on this priceless piece of heritage. She looks again; the tear is grey silk on pink wool, stitched there by the maker. She's been so engrossed in that hollow between lips and chin that she hadn't noticed it. She's studied the nose often enough, marvelling at its modelling; how those weavers conjured the three dimensional from thread. Did she really not notice the tear?

'Lady Munro is a leading speaker for animal rights, though we believe her husband was always closely involved in the local hunt. Much had been made in the press of their opposing views...' The tear has moved into the newly sewn cleft and across the chin. Was Eleanor also a Lady Munro? 'The police have confirmed that they will be searching the lake. Lord Munro has stated he'll give "every possible assistance".'

She studies the photograph. The complete tapestry depicts the passing of time. It tells the story of the hunt and there at the far side, is the other woman, her horse facing back across the landscape.

She turns the handle and releases the rest of the tapestry, gathering up fabric into the middle of the table so that both women are flat on the surface. She swings her light over to shine directly above the second woman and takes up her magnifying glass. The clothes are different, but the face is the same. She's seated on her horse and her right hand is pulling the reigns out towards the viewer, away from her companions and she's smiling a small determined smile.

Looking from one woven lady to the other, across the rucks of fabric she sees that their eyes could meet, a little ivory thread, a little black. She'd like to raise their hands in greeting across the scene acknowledging Eleanor's transition from sadness to courage, but she is conservator, not creator. The news slides into the weather forecast. The heavy rain is at its worst.

She winds the material back until it is taut and flat on the table so only the first Eleanor is visible again. She will work on her eyes after lunch. Nobody will notice, they never do, these slight and secret alterations. She locks and alarms the workroom and walks the cold passage to the kitchen, takes the last of the bread from the freezer and taps the barometer by the back door. It shifts back an inch, almost dead centre. She'll work until six, then make phone calls, send some emails. Perhaps she'll be able to meet up with Maggie at the new wine bar.

The rain on the velux gradually lessens. She phones Maggie and the spell of isolation is broken. She is a woman working across a long bench, earning her living, fulfilling a commission. She applies skills learnt and honed over three decades. So it is something of a shock when she turns the completed section in to the right hand roller revealing the final three feet of the tapestry to find the woman on the horse has faded; her face is suddenly no more than a few frail warp threads. The smile is gone and that assured outward glance. She didn't imagine them, when she looked before lunch, the details were so precise, not just a remembered image, but an image retained in the knowledge of its construction. Her eyes prickle with fatigue. She stretches her fingers and shakes them loose.

The road is flooded, just where it dips by the wisteria-clad cottage. The swollen tidal water has pushed over the bank, but it looks passable. She drives through the water slowly then checks her brakes. She can't get the puzzle of the second Eleanor's face out of her mind and seeks a rational explanation. It will be good to talk to Maggie, to laugh about the strangeness of the disappearing features, of her mind confused by too much solitude and work.

Pressing buttons on the car radio, searching for some music she can sing along to, she catches a snippet of news, '...found drowned in the lake, the police have not ruled out...' As usual the reception disappears as she rounds the bend to climb the hill towards Kingsbridge. It returns as she slows to let a tractor by, but the news is over, the continuity announcer trailing the next programme. She knows, though she wishes she didn't, Lady Munro is dead. Her hands become increasingly clammy as she grips the steering wheel. Part of her wants to turn round, to be back in the studio examining the two Eleanors, comparing the tapestry with the photographs to work out which of the men is the Lady's scheming husband. She won't tell Maggie about the minor alterations she's made. Nor the ones she plans to work on Lord Munro's face.

Introducing Kendra

Gemma Rutter

Monday

Kendra doesn't mind that we have to live upside down. In fact, she prefers it. She likes it that we are fucking, while everyone else is slurping up cornflakes and pretending to read the paper. She likes it that we are holding hands on a damp bench in Regel Street Park while everyone else is trying to find the kettle switch in the dark or reaching for their despondent husbands.

Ice cream tastes the same without sunshine.

On Monday morning Kendra and I wake up fitting with lust. I bite the hem of her nightgown and draw it up over her stomach. She stops me, with the flat of her hand against my receding hairline. 'I want to be able to see you,' she says, and so I get up to push away our red fibre curtains and let the morning in. I press my ear between her breasts and hear the way her heart is getting excited by me. It is at first sleepy, then, realising I am so close, begins to jump and twirl.

Because we live upside down, we don't need foreplay. Kendra and I stamp each other's skin with kisses, but this is unnecessary. Occasionally I part her legs, my fingers tight together like a serpent head and lick at the curve of her thighs with my nails. She likes that. We often perform such things when the other is asleep. Due to the considerate nature of our relationship, should the other appear to be in the midst of a soft dream, we will merely operate quietly and alone.

With the curtains open, we are real to each other in a way not allowed by the darkness. Before we take each other, Kendra demands I curl her hair, the way I do sometimes. She sits before me on the bed, pillows at the small of her back for comfort, and I lift sections of stretched blonde. She wants to be prettier for me, she says, and leans her neck back instinctively towards the heat. At one point she leans back too eagerly, and the tip of the curlers singes her ear lobe. It smells like her perfume.

Within fifteen minutes her head is a mess of corkscrews. She was right, she looks prettier. To hear Kendra purr, I reach my hands over her shoulders and trace her chin, from where it begins, to where it burrows into her neck. She giggles and digs her fingertips into my legs.

Wiggling down into our ruffled bed, Kendra assumes the position; knees agape with her hands curled and loose at her sides, in a way that implies total submission. I work my body next to and over hers, making sure the twists of her hair lay perfectly across her collar bone. I tell Kendra to open her eyes, and press mine against hers as I angle myself in holding her hips. Her mouth opens, and she steals some air sharply. I give her my tongue. Her heart palpitates impossibly fast. To stop myself from coming, I hold tightly to the left side of her face and think about the hands of a clock clicking round. I rub my nose down her cleavage. I alter the pace and depth as I please. I never ask her to guide me; she never offers guidance. We just know what the other wants.

Tuesday

I walk to work with Kev and he tells me about one of his pupils: a small boy seemingly made up of wires. A thin, awkwardly shifting thing who is obsessed with hand painting. He covers his palm in thick red paint and presses it on his Maths book. He covers his palm in thick blue paint and presses it on his English book. Kev says that the boy will obviously become an artist and that anything he can learn from us is therefore a waste of his creative time. I understand this, but I'm also thinking about how silky and cold Kendra's feet are in the morning.

'Tonight,' Kev says, 'Why don't you and Kendra pop round for dinner, like we said? Break out a few bottles.' He winks at me and goes, 'to celebrate.'

Perhaps a celebration is in order. She kept me waiting, panting on her welcome mat for three long weeks. She kept me thirsty with hand-stands up the lounge wall in short skirts, and thoughtful sucking on her lower lip. I revealed to Kev earlier, that on an ordinary Sunday, as we moaned over a cheesy re-run, she had blown hot air in my ear and taken all my clothes. Patience is a beautiful way to be still.

When I get into my classroom, drawings have peeled lazily down above the warm radiator. My messy bunch of children are fighting to get out of rain macs, as parents get them more entangled. I love the names printed above the pegs, the ink swimming in the grooves of the wooden desks, the soft fade of the reading carpet, and all of those flushed, loud faces.

I'm telling them one of my own stories today. Granted, not something I'm allowed to do, but they're bored of the castles and the dragons, and they stick podgy fingers down their throats at the kissing. What these children crave is a heady dose of realism, in a small, safe form. Let's face it I'm never going to be a successful writer. This is as close as I'll ever get to a live reading for my loyal fans. Wiith only four of them asleep, and half the girls plaiting the hair of the other half – this is a very good day indeed. I get to my favourite part in the story. I wouldn't say they were engaged. I wouldn't say they were entertained or interested.

I read, 'And then Emily turned around to find that Ian was gone. He was no longer next to her, or behind her, or even in the church at all. Ian had done a runner and left her alone. Emily would not be getting married.'

I detect a shy wave from someone in the corner, a new girl, whose mother has been rather ambitious in dressing her. She wears a ruffled Victorian blouse, corduroy blue jeans and ruby red slippers with socks. She waves her hand like a soggy white flag. I go, 'Yes?'

She goes, 'Mr, why did he leaves her?'

I go, 'No, leave. He leaves, present. He left, past. But Ian, that's our male character, has just left our female character, Emily.'

I had hoped to end it there, scissor it and continue reading. But one question is a plague on this carpet. They all start coughing them up like crazy. A boy covered head to toe in dog hair goes, 'Do you have a female?'

I go, 'Yes, her name is Kendra.'

A boy wiping down his bottle of cool milk goes, 'Is she pretty?'

I go, 'She's very pretty.'
The first girl goes, 'Is she beautiful?'
I go, 'Very beautiful.'
Dog hair boy goes, 'She will leave then.'
Perhaps my stories are teaching them this. But Kendra won't leave.

Wednesday

The first thing Kev asks me as we shuffle along to the school is this: 'How's Kendra?'

Well, as fine today as she was last night. Normal temperature, no urge to vomit, pale skin not a degree pastier. But for the sake of an already travelling lie, Kendra has to be very sick. 'Throwing up tomato soup until the ring of the toilet bowl was acid green, singed my palm on her forehead, skin bumpy and white like milk just beginning to curdle,' I go.

I imagine that Mrs Kev angrily battered peas simmering in the pan and announced that this was the last time. To be fair, I had found my way out of an astronomical amount of their dinners, with excuses no more believable or credible than this one. Kev is reasonably calm about my last minute cancellation, if not relieved. After a year almost, of never visiting his home, it would be odd behaviour indeed, for me to turn up. He is though, I detect, more curious than ever about Kendra. His initial natural curiosity has sat and boiled in his brain, bubbling up into suspicion. I have known him much longer than her, but still, he is not worthy of my secret.

We spend most of our walk in independent silence. I am thinking heavily on last night, especially the way the damp bench clung to my jeans, especially the way that beer-can struck the curve of her left cheek and cut. Kendra and I had been marvelling at the stars, and the way staring for a long time made them dart about like bright hovercraft. She does love the night. She does not care for the long, scientific names, or for the easy closeness a telescope can bring. It is pure fascination, a need to sit and watch, and feel witness to the dark changes of the universe. I recall that the astronomy book I bought for her, not long after she moved in, we now use for a doorstop. The small, spinning globe I picked out for her at a recent car boot sale, she flicks when bored, merely for the pretty colour of blurred countries and sea.

We had been picking out the stars we'd felt drawn to and sharing them with each other, not uncommon for us of an early Wednesday morning. We expect the odd passer-by; a stumbling student who cannot make us out, unlit and low, a restless tramp searching for a free bench bed, who grumbles at our outlines. But never before a man dressed in a LaCoste tracksuit printed with orange, glow in the dark cockerels. A man drunk enough to approach us, a beer can barely pinched by fingers at his side, but sober enough to be wary of faces he couldn't see. 'Hello there,' he sang, a voice sweet with Carlsberg. 'What ya doing?' he asked. I saw him place a hand firmly at his brow, as if to block out a bright light.

'Nothing. Sitting.' I thought I'd keep it simple, bore him into moving on. I thought my tone would kill his imagination and encourage his feet to start up. I also thought, 'Thank God, for your sake, that I'm not a murderer, a violent stalker, an escaped lunatic. You lucky son of a bitch.'

'Won't mind if I join you then?' And this man advances to Kendra's side and scoots up close to her thigh. 'Don't mind me love.'

She is intimidated. I am threatened. Both of us sit taller, and breathe louder and heat up.

He goes, 'Alright there?' And this man waves one of his big, furry hands in front of her face, and skims the tip of her slightly pointed nose. This rocks her. He almost slips off the edge of the bench. He stands and steps backwards, his trainers sliding through wet leaves. His arm is shaking, and he draws back the can and aims.

We're at the Primary School gates and Kev's looking a bit shifty. He pauses before we go through and says, 'Look, how about tonight? We could come round about eight, grab a take away.'

I'm unprepared. I say, 'That sounds fine.'

Kev's face takes this peculiar shape. He appears to have accomplished something brilliant. The way he sees it, I've already written off Kendra's illness as some twenty-four hour thing. I've already mentioned that Kendra and I planned a quiet evening in with the TV. He has me. That is unless we get broken into, we get bad news about my parents, we get arrested, we fall down the stairs, we fall into the road, we fall down a well, etc. I say to Kev, 'You can come, but don't bring beer.'

Wednesday evening

It's late, and me and Kev huddle in a corner of my kitchen. His breath smells like egg fried rice and Bacardi. He goes, 'She's a bit different to what you said.'

Well, it was last minute. What did he expect? That I'd be able to scoop someone up who mimicked Kendra exactly? The girl, the one in the lounge chatting mindlessly to Mrs Kev, she used to baby-sit my nephew. I had offered to pay her extra, should she allow me to dye her hair honey blonde, but she'd shaken her brown curls at me.

'She dyed her hair this afternoon,' I say.

He says, 'You said she was pale.'

'So she got a tan.'

'You said she was from here.'

'She puts on an accent when she's nervous. She's young, it's a defensive thing,' I say.

The babysitter is right this second explaining a reality TV show in thick Scottish. Sure, her eyebrows are brown, her arm hair is brown. She is deeply tanned, with wide olive strap lines over her shoulders.

'That's Kendra,' I go.

We venture back into the lounge and sit protectively beside our drinks. Both women ignore us and continue swapping stories. The babysitter is speaking of our rather romantic first date. She has me being incredibly strange, awkwardly so. She has me make the first move, and her, at first, decline. The story stays loyal to an A/B structure. A, sees her mention something critical about me. B, sees her appearing in some beautiful way. Let me show you:

A: *He had very sweaty hands.*
B: *I didn't mind watching that war film he loved.*
A: *He expected me to go all the way with him.*
B: *I shared my popcorn and let him have the last bit.*

A: *He commented that my dress was a little long.*
B: *I phoned him to arrange a second date.*

Occasionally, she throws in a combined A/B:

A/B: *I offered to buy dinner, he let me.*

They're obvious lies. They're words from the girl who has longed for the spotlight her whole life, then, finally under it, splutters and blushes and messes it all up. Kev looks at me the whole time, pupils high up in his eyes. He eats the salted peanuts rapidly and utters a deep 'Uh-huh' every few sentences. Mrs Kev excuses herself to go to the toilet. The babysitter isn't fussed. She just wants an audience. She starts talking to me about the first time we made love, about clothes getting caught, my initial impotence and her frustrating lack of orgasm. Then, the story evidently climaxes and she confides, 'And after all that, I still went back.'

The babysitter squeezes my knee and my knee hates her. Then, a scream, surprisingly loud, when the walls of my house are so thick. A stampede down the stairs and Mrs Kev is screeching in the middle of my lounge, 'What is that? What is it?'

Kev stands up. 'What? Calm down love.'

She pushes him away. 'I will not. There's something upstairs in his bed. Some giant, bloody, doll.'

Kev winks. 'Teddies at your age mate.'

She spits at him, 'No, you idiot. It has breasts, and this body. It's all made-up with this, with this underwear, and a face.'

They start really yelling at each other then. He thinks she's embarrassing and had way too much to drink. She thinks he's not listening and had way too much to drink.

I go: 'Excuse me, you're both incredibly rude. Kendra's trying to sleep.'

My cousin who could catch flies and tickle fish with his bare hands

Mark Czanik

Aunty Marge thought I was funny. Sometimes she had only to look at me and she would laugh. 'You tickles me,' she'd say. She never told me why, but whatever it was she found to laugh at, I never felt a fool because of it. It was strange because everybody else said Aunty Marge had a terrible temper. Dad used to talk about it in the car on our way to Ashberry, although I only once had occasion to witness it for myself. Aunty Marge was mum's older sister, and although mum didn't live in the country any more, they were still close. I knew without touching that their hair felt the same.

In the summer holidays I used to go and stay at Aunty Marge's. Burrow Court was a black and white house at the bottom of a dell. The walls were bumpy and crooked, and the stairs so steep you sometimes had to crawl up on your hands and knees just to stop from falling backwards. It was often cold in that house, even in summer, but when Uncle Leonard lit the fire the living room became so warm your whole body felt heavy and sleepy; it was as much as you could do to raise an arm. Behind the settee, my cousin Dan and I raced cotton reels primed with elastic bands and matchsticks, which would crawl like miniature turtles across the carpet.

There was no running water at Burrow Court. Whenever Aunty Marge wanted water she had to get it from the pump. She'd go outside and pump the handle and after a while water would gush out. There was also a water-butt in the garden. Aunty Marge told me never to go anywhere near that water-butt in case I fell in and drowned and she had to tell my mother, but it was hard not to disobey her sometimes and pull myself up because when I peeked over the top, I could see Thunderbirds 2 and 4 floating inside.

There were three sheds in the garden.

The first shed wasn't a shed at all, but an outhouse. When you couldn't hold it any longer that's where you had to go. I used to feel like a condemned man on my way there. The actual toilet looked like a real one, but it was just a hole. I won't even mention the spiders and flies. The only good thing about it was going after dark because then, even though it was spooky, you got to use Uncle Leonard's torch. You could sit on the seat and play Mysterons, or if you left the door open the beam would reach all the way to the Kennards' on the other side of the lane.

Next to that was Uncle Leonard's shed. That was always padlocked, so I never discovered exactly what was in there, but every so often a Tudor dolls house would appear on the kitchen table, or a little gypsy wagon with proper wheels and tiny people inside.

The third shed was the best. That was where Dan kept his animals. Dan, as I've said, was my cousin. He was three and a half years older than me and could catch flies with his bare hands. He could also tickle fish and skip stones a record twenty-three times across the moat. It was impossible to think of Dan as ever having to go to school.

There were two types of animals in his shed. The first type were live animals, and the second were stuffed. There were stuffed jackdaws, and stuffed crows, and stuffed jenny wrens and jays. If ever I went into the shed by myself, I was convinced those birds were staring at me when my back was turned, especially the barn owl whose mustard eyes seemed to follow me everywhere.

The live animals were mostly ferrets. Sometimes I tried holding them, but I hated how they wriggled and shivered in my hands, their hearts beating so fast. It was obvious they loved Dan, the way they scurried up and down his legs, and sat on his shoulders and kissed his teeth.

The best thing about the third shed, though, were the weapons. Dan had a whole arsenal. He had two air rifles, an air pistol, a set of telescopic sights, a crossbow, two bow-and-arrows, and three or four catapults of his own design. He had knives too; not just penknives, but sheath knives, skinning knives, buck knives – you name it. I liked the guns best of all.

All I had at home was a spud gun and a toy Winchester.

Ashberry was the real thing. Set the cans up on the compost heap, kneel on the path with a tin of ammo between you and the trough for an arm-rest, and it wasn't hard to pretend you were *Trinity* or *The Man with No Name*.

Dan shot the birds himself. Often he got me to aim at them, but somehow I never quite managed it, despite the fact that I was good with the ·22 and could take the pink head off a matchstick.

My cousin was full of stories. Not just the usual stuff about headless chickens and decapitated eels, but other more puzzling facts. For example, he told me that if you set an ice-cube on the ground, an ant will circle it exactly three times in an anti-clockwise direction before it dies; that snakes go blind while shedding their skins; that geese circle their home three times clockwise before forming a V pattern and leaving. I tried the trick with the ice-cube a few times on my own and I was always on the lookout for snakes down the moat or geese circling overhead, but these things only seemed to work properly when Dan was around.

*

Dan and I were in the shed with the stuffed birds. I liked the smell of it in there, which was mainly straw and sawdust, but mixed in with something else, like bruised apples turned over in the grass. We'd been in there for ages, not saying very much, when suddenly he said, 'Why don't you ask Wicky for a fight?'

Wicky was what he called our cousin, after his surname, Whitchurch, but I didn't know him that well, so just called him Adrian.

'Why?' I asked.

'I'm sure you could beat him up.'

I quite liked Adrian. He had a go-cart he used to push me in around his dad's vegetable patch, even though I knew he wanted me to crash.

'Have you ever had a fight with him?' I said.

'Loads of times.'

'Is he hard?'

'Wicky! Wicky's a weakling. Everyone knows that. Why don't you go and ask him for a fight? You're a great fighter.'

'Do you think so?'

'Yeah.'

'How do you know?'

'I can tell from just looking at you.'

I was happy playing with the ferrets, but he kept going on about it, saying what a great fighter I was and how easy it would be, so in the end I said okay. 'Where is he?' I asked, hoping he didn't know.

'Down at the pavilion, watching his dad play cricket.'

I hesitated. I'd never been to the pavilion before and there would be adults.

'Go on, it's not far.'

'Where is it again?'

He told me where to go: up Roman Road, past the Village Hall, ten minutes down Tilly Lane 'til you get to the stile. Really, it wasn't far.

It took ages to get there; walking always takes longer when you're on your own. Eventually, though, I saw the big white hut with the green diagonal beams Dan had described, and the men playing cricket. I sat on the stile, watching. I couldn't see Adrian anywhere. It was a stupid idea anyway; I could be practising the pellet gun now. Then just as I was about to turn back, I saw him. I wished I hadn't. He was by the pavilion, playing football with a couple of boys. I slid off the stile, climbed the gate into the next field. Every now and then I peered through the hedge. It was definitely Adrian. He didn't sound very tough, although it was hard to tell from just his voice. When I got quite close I sat on the grass. I sat there ages, wondering what to do.

Then Adrian was looking straight towards me. 'Who's that?'

I froze.

'There's someone sitting behind that hedge.'

The other two boys looked towards the hedge. 'Where?' the first one said.

'There!' he said, pointing.

'Oh, yeah!'

'Where? I can't see,' said the second one.

'There, look, follow my finger.'

'Oh, yeah.'

'Who's that?' Adrian called out.

I said nothing.

'Who's that sitting behind that hedge?' Slowly, as if I was some kind of bird that might fly off if they moved too fast, they started walking towards me. 'Who is it?' Adrian said, as if to himself. Then, 'It's Grant!' he said.

Something like a tiny electric shock passed through my spine.

'Is that you, Grant?'

'Who's Grant?' the first boy said.

'It's my cousin.'

'Your cousin?'

'Yeah, my cousin! It's my bloody cousin!'

'What's he doing sitting behind that hedge?'

'I dunno, what you asking me for?' He came closer. 'Is that you, Grant?'

A cry went up from the cricketers, followed by a smattering of applause. 'Yes,' I said.

'What you doin' there?'

'Nothing. Just sittin'.'

'Have you been there long?'

I pulled at the grass. They were all staring. Adrian was holding the ball. It looked like a good ball – real leather, plenty of air in it, not too light. Then he said, 'Do you wanna come and 'ave a game of footy with us?' Adding to the boys, 'Grant's good at footy, he plays all the time…You play all the time, don't you, Grant?'

'Quite a bit.'

'You play for County now, don't you?'

'Yeah.' I didn't, and I had the feeling he knew I didn't, but it was a nice thing to say anyway.

'Yeah, come and 'ave a game.'

'Is there a way in?'

'You'll have to go back the way you came.'

I walked back along the hedge and came down the other side. Soon I was dribbling and dummying and back-heeling it past the keeper; I had to show off a bit because they thought I played for County. Adrian ran after me, chipping at my heels. He wasn't as good as me, but he was better than he looked. Afterwards we had tea in the pavilion with the cricketers. Uncle Ron and Uncle Frank were there. Women too, who seemed to have come from nowhere, serving food and pouring drinks and smiling in their nice flowery dresses. I was shy because I didn't know anybody my age except Adrian, but everyone was friendly and no-one seemed surprised I was there. We all sat around the two long wooden tables eating and drinking and laughing in the big airy room with the doors wide open, and the sun streaming down through the high windows, and I didn't think about Dan once.

*

A few days later I was in the kitchen with Dan, eating blackberry and apple crumble, which was Aunty Marge's speciality, when the phone rang. Straight away I knew it was mum. Dan handed me the phone and I stood there, holding it to my ear. We didn't have a telephone at home so I had no idea where she was calling from. 'Hello, Grant,' she said in her singsong voice.

I told her about all the target practice I'd been doing, and the huge carp I'd caught with Dan. It was strange because I felt sad telling her, as if it hadn't been as much fun doing these things as I'd first thought.

'You be careful with those guns, won't you.'

'I am.'

'Poor little birds.'

Mum said that, but she kept a jackdaw when she was a girl that used to follow her around everywhere because she clipped its wings. She'd taught it to talk too. When one day she found it floating in the water-butt, old Kennard told her it must have seen its own reflection in the water and gone down after it and drowned, but she always insisted he did it because the bird had taken to chatting outside his window every morning.

'Your sisters are on the land this week. They've been working eversahard.'

'Oh,' I said.

'They've been up early, and making their own sandwiches. They're gone all day.'

'Has Amber been doin' it, too?'

'Well, aye! She's a good little picker.'

I felt sad then. When I put the phone down I couldn't eat my pudding. Dan took me shooting down the moat. On the way we had to walk along Roman Road. Every now and then a lorry would rush past blasting hot fuggy air. We had to climb the narrow bank next to the ditch and balance there to stop from being sucked in. I felt so small, even holding the gun. I tried to stop Dan from seeing my face.

'What's the matter?' he said.

'It's not fair. I'm stuck 'ere, and my sisters are earnin' all that money.'

'So?'

'Nobody told me they'd be workin'.' A red car swished past. Somewhere a magpie was rattling like a toy machine-gun. 'I en't got no money.'

'What do you need money for?'

I didn't have an answer to that.

'Oh, you're such a towny sometimes.'

'I'm not.'

'You are.'

We walked on in silence for a while, hugging the ditch.

'Oh, stop crying!' he said.

But I couldn't, I couldn't shake the sadness off, and all that day, and the next day too, I was miserable.

*

Later that week we were mucking about with the earth-roller, trying to flatten a dead rat, when Dan had an idea.

'Let's bury each other!'

'Yeah!'

So we began digging a hole in the vegetable plot. It took hours to finish; Uncle Leonard's spades were heavy and it was difficult splicing the blade into the earth to begin with, but we worked hard, in a kind of frenzy in the piping hot sun. By the time we finished the sky was streaked with red. We stood admiring our work. It was a good hole. Dan got some boards from the pigsty and laid them over the top. He looked at me, face smudged with dirt, eyes gleaming.

'Get in, then.'

'Me?'

'Go on, you'll be fine. Get in and I'll pull the boards over, and cover it with soil. Then I'll go and tell mum you're lost.'

'Will I be able to breathe?'

'Course, I'll leave a breathing hole.'

'What about spiders?' He rolled his eyes. I didn't want him to start calling me a weed like he did Wicky, so I jumped into the hole and manoeuvred myself under the boards.

'Ready?' he said.

'Ready,' I said. I was trying not to giggle. I had to admit it was a brilliant idea. He drew the boards over. It was dark. Cold, too; I only had my Mighty Dynamo tee shirt on. He began covering the surface. The boards shook violently every time a clod of earth landed on them, like little explosions going off. Soon after, I heard him raking over the soil. He seemed to take ages over that. Then he was looking down at me through a tiny peep hole – I could see his eye.

'Okay?' he whispered.

'Yeah,' I whispered back. 'Does it look good?'

'It looks great. If you didn't know, you'd have no idea there was a hole here.'

'Really?'

'Yeah.'

'Amazing.'

'Can you breathe okay?'

'Just about. It's really dark in here, though.'

He didn't answer at first. Then, 'Is it?' he said.

'Can you get me the torch?'

'I'll go and get mum first. When you hear her calling don't answer at first, then start moaning. You're really good at that.'

I heard footsteps receding, then nothing. I lay there, eyes latched onto the chink of light. Sometime after, I heard Aunty Marge calling my name. I didn't answer at first, but by the fifth or sixth time she was beginning to sound a bit cross. I gave a whoop, then waited, hand clamped to my mouth.

Nothing. I let out another whoop, this time louder.

'*Hey, I'm here.*'

A rook cawed like a creaking door.

'*Aunty Marge…*'

My voice sounded blunt and echoless.

'*Come and get me.*'

No reply. The earth smelt thick and heavy. I lay there, darkness pressing in on me. Nothing seemed to be happening, so I put my hand up and pushed at the board. It was surprisingly heavy. I pushed harder. The board rose up an inch and splinters of light poured in. I caught a glimpse of grey sky, purple cloud, before the board slapped down again. Specs of dirt fell onto my face, into my mouth. Something feathery brushed against my hand. I heard a grinding noise next to my ear, like tiny jaws. Then I began to scream.

*

Dad came and took me home the next day, but I was back the following weekend because he had to do some work for Aunty Marge. He was helping them dig a trench from the top of the garden down to the house. Soon there would be running water at Burrow Court and Aunty Marge wouldn't have to use the pump any more. Dan helped dig as well. Dad and he worked with their shirts off while I sat in the apple tree watching from the shade.

Now they'd both washed themselves under the pump and had their shirts on again.

'Get down from there now,' dad called up.

'We're going now,' mum called soon after.

But I didn't want to get down; there were loads more apples to pick. Plus, Dan had promised to get the crossbow out and he'd obviously forgotten. The only reason I'd got out of the hole alive had been because Aunty Marge had finally heard my screams.

Dad came out of the house again. 'Grant, I won't tell you again!'

I climbed down and went indoors. There were voices coming from the kitchen, so I went into the living room. I sat by the hearth and stabbed the ashes with the poker. Then I looked through some of Dan's *Spider-Man* comics. He didn't have many, hardly any compared to my collection, but he did have one I didn't have: issue #62, April 1974, *Spider-Man vs the Vulture*. It was only a British reprint, but I still wanted it. I liked the Vulture. He's bald, and curiously old and skinny looking for a villain. He's also incredibly strong and always escaping from prison. And of course he can fly whenever he has his bird costume. I thought of taking it, but I knew Dan would notice it was missing. There was a screwdriver in the grate. I pushed it into the sheepskin rug for a while, but nothing really happened. There was a low stool by the armchair, the seat made out of hop twine. The pattern was four triangles meeting in the middle at a point. I positioned the screwdriver between the top layers of the weave of one of the triangles and pushed. It went in easily, so I kept pushing until I felt something snap. It was a satisfying sound, like the click of an anorak stud slotting into place. I pushed the blade in again, this time another triangle. I pushed and twisted, pushed and twisted, until I felt another thread snap.

I examined the stool. You couldn't tell it was broken, not unless you knew first. If you studied it from a certain angle it even looked improved. I did it again four or five times, and then I heard dad calling.

*

The next time we went to Ashberry, Aunty Marge was hanging sheets out on the washing line when we arrived. There had been a gale the night before. It was still blustery and the trees had lost their leaves. I jumped out of the car and sauntered up to her doing one of my walks. She didn't laugh when she saw me. She didn't even say hello. 'Don't you come near me!' she said.

I stopped at the edge of the lawn with the sheets snapping between us.

'You little bugger! I could tan your ass for you.'

At first I couldn't remember what I'd done.

'Comin' 'ere, as if butter wouldn't melt in your mouth.'

Then I knew.

'You wicked boy.'

I went and hid in the pigsty. For the rest of the day Aunty Marge didn't say another word to me, not even when we were on our way to the car. I sat in the back waiting for everyone. I hadn't seen Dan all day, and I wanted to get going in case I did. There was a new stereo in the boot, our first, and mum had bought us each a record. Mine was *Big Western Movie Themes*, with a picture of two gunfighters on the cover.

I didn't wave as we pulled away.

'Why did you do that to Daniel's stool?' mum said as soon as we were out of sight. 'That took him ages to make, that stool. He put a lot of work into that.'

I slid down behind the record. There was 'Gunfight at the O.K. Corral', 'A Fistful of Dollars', 'The Good, the Bad and the Ugly.'

'You've ruined it now.'

I didn't know what to say.

'You broke his little heart, you did.'

Dad said nothing, Jane said nothing; even Amber was quiet.

'Oh, why did you do it?' mum said after a long silence.

We passed an old tree that had come down during the storm. Through the gaps in the hedge, I could see kids clambering over it and I thought of Gulliver tied down by the little people in his sleep.

Later that year, Aunty Marge and Uncle Leonard moved out of the black and white house into the schoolhouse up the road. The new house had all the latest mod cons, but none of the things I loved so much about Burrow Court. There was no garden, no cliff staircase, and the windows rattled in their frames whenever lorries went past. I looked for the ferrets and the stuffed birds and the air-rifles in the new shed, but couldn't find them anywhere. Dan drove a motorbike now, Adrian had one too, and I hardly saw either of them any more.

Whenever we visited we could still see the old black and white house down in the dell as we drove along the long straight road through Ashberry, but I never went there again.

Little Things

Eleanor Knight

Audrey had pigeons. 'It's the mess!' she said, peering up from the back of Jim's car, 'The front porch looks awful. People will think I'm the Grundys. Look at it!'

Jim parked up against the curb, leaving the engine running.

'Like I said', said Jim 'No point in leaving it. You'll just have to get rid. Vermin.'

He swung his head slowly from side to side over the steering wheel, looking like a gored bull. The doctor had advised gentle exercise for his neck.

'Aren't they wood pigeons?' said Cynthia. 'I thought you said they were.'

'Same difference, Cynth love,' he said, from the bottom of a slow rotation, 'Rats on the wing.'

Cynthia pulled a face. Last autumn a pair of shrews had got in and tampered with the chutney, torn right through the cellophane tops and gorged themselves, she could swear there were tiny tunnels where they'd dug in with their noses. She'd washed the pantry floor twice and still wondered.

'Any luck on the house front?'

Audrey rolled her eyes. 'Not a sausage. It's all very tiring. A bad time, apparently.'

'When isn't?' said Jim, darkly.

Cynthia threw him a look from the passenger seat. 'Never mind, Aud' she said. 'It only takes one. It's such a lovely big house.'

'Cynth,' said Jim

'Oh, don't worry,' Audrey unplugged her seatbelt and opened the door. 'It's too big for me.'

Cynthia and Jim had been wonderful; kept her in the swim, as they said, though still holding back their familiar smiles so that their lips looked like the rims of unbaked pies.

'Same time next week' called Jim as he pulled away. 'Look after yourself. If there's anything you need…'

Audrey waved and turned to go in. There they were marching up and down on top of the roof, twitch-headed, making the wobbling noise she so hated to wake up to. One of them was making a fuss of herself on top of the chimney. Audrey had a vision of Cynthia in a fitting room. Poor Cynthia, she made a lot of flapjacks for her grandchildren who didn't necessarily like them.

Everyone said it would be all the little things; turning the light out whenever she liked, no waiting to read the newspaper, finding everything exactly where she last put it. Yesterday she'd even bought a new CD, something from Cuba, and played it loudly all evening with the French doors open while she did the weeding. This year she would eat the broad beans while they were still tiny and put all the runners out on the drive with an honesty box. It was an odd kind of freedom, nothing to celebrate, fretted away at the edges by guilt in case she caught herself enjoying it, and meanwhile people were still saying they were 'So sorry to hear…': no-one ever finished the sentence, it sounded ridiculous. Seventy one years and a trite little rhyme at the end of it: 'Guy died.' In the last weeks of his illness when everyone knew, the few people she actually saw said it was no age these days. She would get a rush of vertigo, her husband's life like a long cane and she balancing on the top of it, an acrobat, looking down.

When, a lifetime ago, she had announced Guy one evening over the washing up, running him up like a flag, her mother had said, 'Ten years isn't nothing you know, not at your age.' Audrey, capped-sleeved and twenty, couldn't have cared less. Here was a man who had qualified as a doctor while she was still sewing aprons at school, drove a sports car and, on the single occasion that he came, at his own suggestion, to tea with her parents, had shaved so exquisitely that she couldn't help herself from cupping her hands around his delicately scented face. Audrey looked forward very much to discovering the difference in the decade between them.

Their honeymoon was to be in Dieppe, 'The closest beach to Paris!' Audrey's mother told the neighbours, hoping to hide her disappointment, only it wasn't. 'Someone had blundered' Guy joked afterwards, though Audrey wasn't sure about the allusion as applied to the beginning of their married life. A series of delays and missed connections saw the newlyweds stranded on the emptying platform at Lewes, in the blazing heat of a sun that, having missed the wedding, had caught up with them en route, and like a rude guest, now bore down on the happy couple, pressing on them a gift that needed opening straight away. What had been Audrey's darling two-piece in oyster white with matching veiled pillbox at eleven o'clock in Kensal Rise, was at seven o'clock on this June evening after a long journey, too tight, too itchy and, Audrey was sure, full of confetti in places she wasn't going to explore in public. Above all she longed to take her off her shoes.

'Come on!' Guy took her hand and pulled her after the trail of people walking uphill into the town.

'Bound to be somewhere up here. Only for one night' he said. Audrey gripped her suitcase, not daring to look at where it might be snagging her stockings. One night. The back of her neck prickled.

'What a view!' she said at the top, putting her case down for a moment. The winged Victory in the middle of the High Street seemed to be proclaiming nothing less than the sheer beauty of its surroundings, the glorious jumble of shop-fronts, tile and timber hunkering over the brow of the hill and dropping down towards the river below, and just beyond, seemingly at the end of the street, the Downs loomed velvet green under the triumphant blue sky. Perfectly framed, she thought, a wedding present. 'Mmm…' said Guy, 'Round as a barmaid's thighs.' He turned his back and led the way to the hotel.

Their rooms – for the manageress was charmed by Audrey's childlike attempt to sign her new surname with a flourish – included a rather grand sitting room, with long sash windows onto the street, its walls hung with a collection of hunting scenes and a deer's head, pitted with moth holes above the fireplace, all gave it the forbidding air of a gentleman's club. In contrast, their bedroom and the little dressing room, all in eau de nil and fresh white linen, gave a zesty air of innocence that only the best hotel laundries can maintain.

They changed, splashed their faces with cold water and walked out, down through the town and along the river. It was cooler now. ('You walked until *what* time?' Audrey's mother had demanded, outraged.) Midges taunted them in small clouds here and there along the path; in the distance a church tower rose a little way above the trees, the river wound lazily ahead of them, a swan dropped its white neck straight down like a plumb line beneath the darkening surface. The frantic beating of wings above made them look up as an elegant pair of grey collared doves curved gracefully towards the woodland on the opposite bank before plunging with indecorous haste into the plush embrace of an oak.

Guy put his arm around her shoulders and steered her silently back towards the town.

Funny that she could remember it all so vividly when now, for example, (and it was age, she supposed) she could read two thirds of a novel before realising she'd read it before, struggled with the names of new babies, forgot the most important item on even the shortest shopping list – and they were all, now, short. There had been a time when all the details had been there, something to delight in, a cheerful jar of buttons she could sift through her fingers, poring over their colours and shapes, remembering where they had all belonged.

'You're so good at going with the flow' Guy used to say. 'That's what you're good at.' She'd talked him through troubles at work, encouraged him to take up hobbies, made space for him, time. Had it all been enough? Had *she* been enough? What was left of her now?

Of course she had meant to wait for him. She had left him sunk in one of the deep leather sofas, cultivating a chivalrous interest in a clothy pile of Country Life while she bathed. The ceremony, the fuss with the sandwiches and the top tier of the cake almost falling over because the little plaster pillars had sunk into the icing, her sweet bridesmaids – putting Cynthia in charge had made up for *her* disappointment – so full of smiles, the endless handshakes and kisses, all afternoon women dabbing away smears of their lipstick apologetically from her cheek; the final getaway, as Guy called it, in a taxi and then the train so delayed stop after stop all the way from Victoria, such a long, long day, not to mention the heat, and now here she was, lying between the coolest of sheets in a hotel bedroom, and Guy, her husband, she could see him through the open doorway, jigging his foot in time to an imaginary tune.

She fell asleep.

She walked up the empty drive, unlocked the garage door and swung it up and over. Guy's car, shrouded with a mildewed tarpaulin, lay to one side surrounded by lawnmower parts, a wooden stepladder on its side, an empty milk crate, cardboard boxes she didn't even want to look in, a few planks. She picked her way through the junk and ran her hand over the makeshift shelves; rusted tins of Swarfega, one or two cans of paint she shook just to hear the ball bearings rattle, brushes, screwdrivers, a set of sparkplugs thrown into a carrier bag. The cracked, yellow door of one of their old kitchen cupboards hung open slightly on the back wall. She reached inside and brought down Guy's old air-rifle and a tobacco tin of lead pellets. Holding the mahogany stock under her arm, as she'd watched him do so many times, she drew the barrel down slowly towards her until she felt the click and, taking a pellet from the tin, pressed it home, cool and soft, greasy almost, under her thumb. Something about the colour of it – too much to hope that she would remember what – that pale, smooth grey, made her feel she would weep.

Outside, Audrey stepped back onto the edge of the front lawn and took aim.

Reef

Jane Draycott

From this height the reef looks like an emerald snakeskin, as if she might reach down and touch it. In the lagoon the stilt village appears tiny, a matchstick model, the shallow water beneath each house a blaze of gold and blue. She has the crazy thought that the inhabitants might be able to see her looking down at them. Perhaps one of the young fishermen. But even if he saw her and shouted, she wouldn't be able to understand a word he'd say.

'Sophie!' She hasn't even had two minutes' rest. '*Il conto per tavola sette!*' Nico is calling across the cafe at her. 'Table seven wants their bill.' Her heart races again.

She looks away from the calendar, which is hung above the bar between the antique ice-skates and the till. It is a present from Nico's son, an airline engineer. Last month it was a fish-market in West Africa – February: piles of slithering fish spilled out on the dirty tarmac, unsold, forever waiting for someone to come and take them away.

The old lady on table seven is raising her eyebrows at Sophie, writing her signature in the air. She has red hair which is a kind of cloud-colour at the roots, like a mix of fire and vapour. After she pays, Sophie accompanies her out to the street.

'Come again.' She watches the old woman totter down the snow-packed pavement towards the bus. Nico says she was a collaborator. 'Bye. Come again.' Though perhaps by then Sophie will have gone.

Each time someone pays and leaves, her chest contracts a little. This month is the worst so far. She returns to the bar and begins polishing glasses gently, to bring her heart-beat down. She looks again at the photo of the reef. March. In the corner of the picture a small boat speeds away towards the open sea along a channel carved in the coral. A single route in and out. In the distance the ocean looks stony and cold.

A young lad has come in leaving the door open so the morning air streams in like an icy river round everyone's feet. 'Hey - don't they even teach you how to close a door these days?' Nico is a kind man but his tone frightens the boy, who blushes, rooted to the spot. In her first week Nico tried to touch her up, to feel her breast as she stood polishing glasses. She'd screamed, a short quiet scream, and that was that. Now he's only ever kind to her.

She goes to the open door, takes in the freezing air streaming down from the peaks. She can hear the post-office helicopter swinging around somewhere on the other side of the valley, though she can't see it against the whitened chequerboard of meadow and forest. As she closes the door the wind takes it and slams it.

'Sorry,' says the boy as she passes back around him.

He is what her mother would have called a lovely lad, colouring up like a girl. He has the kind of face that's like a new laid snow-field and goes about the world like a reproach to all the marks others will make on it. The kind of boy who used to fancy her, although she never fancied them.

'Don't worry,' she smiles. 'So, hot chocolate?' As she steams the milk she looks again at the stilt village, the sheltered water, the passage out through the sharp coral.

Edward had been the exception, a lovely lad who wasn't like a girl. The smell of the milk rises towards her face and for a second she is in Devon, in the kitchen watching her mother make custard. From infant school she and Ed moved in the same group of friends, fluid, easy, grouping and regrouping like birds or fish. Then their vodka-fuelled kiss on the college trip to Sicily opened some other door, like the dream she still has sometimes in which she speaks a brand new language all night long.

Customers are beginning to come in for lunch on their way up or down from the pass. Delivery drivers, tourists, couples on weekend trips. The blushing boy has taken his drink and is standing watching the soundless TV – an aerial view of the skiing. One after another the competitors throw themselves down the mountain in their variegated colours rippling down the snow-covered rock.

Volunteering together was as inevitable as if it had been marked in an almanac, the posting in east Africa yet another in their set of lucky cards. They arrived in the season of clear skies, driven from the airstrip by the Headmaster in his battered car down an astonishing avenue of flame-trees that led to their bungalow. For three years, protected by the perimeter fence, this was their world. Once a week they went off down the single sand-road to get beer and supplies. In the evenings they did their marking and learnt Swahili beside the kerosene lamp while the students sat it out with their books and candles in the mosquito-filled dormitories.

She empties the glass-washer and peers to look closer at the reef. It almost has the lizard-look of the chagreen cigarette case left to her by her godmother long before she was old enough to smoke. Her aunt must have died young, though then she had seemed old. Chagreen. She hadn't even known the word.

The safari was their end-of-tour treat. They travelled across the border to meet their red-haired guide and the nine other tourists. At first the landscape looked like Switzerland in summer – sloping-roofed chalets and grassy meadows. But soon they reached the rainforest and the mist, and the world changed. Even the acoustic of their voices inside the minibus.

The restaurant is filling up now, noisy and hot. The blushing boy has gone. It is all she can do to keep up with the drinks orders and clearing plates. The husbands and wives at their tables stare at their food and out of the window and sometimes at each other.

They'd been given the small tent behind the main dormitory tent. Woken in the dark, they'd sat bolt upright listening to violent shouting coming from the ranger's post. At the first round of gunfire Sophie screamed. Within seconds they were out and running, heading for the latrine block. They locked themselves into a cubicle and froze. A gecko ran down the wall beside her knee. When the first soldier kicked down the door, she screamed again.

'Shut up!' Ed yelled. He sounded like somebody she didn't know.

During the forced march up through the forest she walked close behind him, often treading on his heels. Each time she slipped or lost her footing, her pulse leapt and the sweat fountained from her. Eventually the sliding became a rhythm of its own. No-one talked. When they all stopped, the two of them crouched together as if they were a single body.

'Bill for table five!' Nico is almost shouting now and her heart begins to pound.

She puts the last of the glasses back on the shelf. What isn't clear from the photograph is how the inhabitants of the stilt village come and go from their houses. Apart from the single craft speeding away through the coral there are no other boats. No jetties, no ladders down from the doorways. Perhaps they are all out fishing. Perhaps they have drawn up the ladders.

The soldiers argued in front of everyone about the four American women in the group. They spoke in something that sounded like Kiswahili, though there was barely a word she understood. One boy with pock-marked skin pushed at the teenage girl, then in a single brutal movement put his rifle to the head of the oldest woman, whose daughter started to cry.

'Stop it! Stop it please.'

The boy with the gun lowered it toward the ground. The commander shouted in a strangulated voice to two other soldiers, who took the four women back down the path they'd just hacked through.

When they stopped again, it was almost dark. Three others were taken back down the path, including the Canadian student they'd talked to in the bus. Sophie knew she might die. She had lost control of her body – every last inch of effort went into trying to breathe calmly to stop herself shaking violently. Ed was white, immobile, barely breathing, like a block of stone beside her.

The lunch clients have nearly all gone. She re-sets the tables. Someone pushes the door wide open from the street. She smells the slush and diesel of the darkening afternoon as Jacopo swings heavily down the step on his sticks. He survived the camps but his useless hip surgeon has finally done for his love life, he says. 'Hello, my lovely.' He's come early for the card game. 'You make sure he gives you a proper lunch break, or he'll have me to answer to.' He waves his stick and laughs loudly.

She clears the table by the stove and gets the cards. For a second she hears the helicopter again. Building materials. Or the ambulance lift. She is tired and not sure now if she'll make it to the end of her shift.

She'd climbed the path as if disembodied, watching herself from above. At one point, she thought perhaps she had already been killed. Then everything except the noise of the birds stopped. A hand pushed at her head. The soldier who'd been behind them all the way forced up and past them. The tour guide was slithering back down towards them, a piece of paper in his hand. 'Don't say a thing. Walk back down. Don't look up.' A note for the US Ambassador. The soldiers had gone on up without them. It was now that she felt the wind on her face: the top, the border.

'I'll just have a small one today,' Jacopo sits with his legs splayed awkwardly out in front of him. Twenty four hours later in the sanctuary of the High Commission they learned what the rest of the world already knew. The four American women had been found, hacked to death with axes and machetes, the teenager raped first. There were notes attached to their bodies. 'This is your punishment.' The three men were still missing.

She barely has the energy now to pull on the pump. The glass fills like a slow incoming wave. From the airport, they'd gone separately to their families. The flashbacks came mostly at night, the pock-marked boy, the crouching fear in the latrines, the screaming daughter. Sometimes she walked on the cliff, hunched. At not being braver, at being lucky. Her mother, she knew, followed her at a distance. For three days Ed didn't reply to her texts or answer the phone. When he came to the house, they were strangers. Two weeks later he said they had to go back, to pick up the thread.

Each time the door opens she thinks it might be him. But she knows where he is, thousands of miles beyond the mountains, somewhere she can only envisage at the end of a long lens.

She couldn't put her mother through it. It was all she could do to persuade her that she'll be safe here, in this backwater of a village which every new month she vows she must leave. Held to the spot as if someone had shouted at her to wait, to explain herself.

It is completely dark outside now. The bar is filling up again. The mountain rescue team are in, crowded round the TV after training. Nico turns up the volume: local news, a protest against the selling-off of social housing, an interview with a conservation officer about the re-appearance of wolves in the region.

She looks again at the calendar, lifts the photo of the reef to get a glimpse of next month. April. A dark green maze in the gardens of a French château. At its heart a small square of grass which looks cool and velvety. Like all the other photos, the silent worlds seen from the air, it's hard to tell whether what she's looking at is very far or very close.

Ed still writes as if they were just apart for a while, and always asks when she will come. Soon the rescue team will start on their second beers and the talk will turn as it has done every night this week to the men who died in last year's avalanche. The companions they describe as lost, as if one day they might go back and find them again somewhere out among the meadows and forest.

Yusef

Graham Mort

When Marie came up with Pendeen as a holiday venue, I must have looked surprised, so that curious look came over her face. Well, I *was* surprised. I hadn't been there for over thirty years. Which made me feel old, to say the least.

'Pendeen? How do you spell that?'

She looked surprised now, squinting at the map. We were having breakfast and the kitchen table was scattered with coffee cups and plates. The gas boiler was grumbling and there were a pair of greenfinches upside-down on the bag of nuts she'd hung from the washing line.

'P-e-n-d-e-e-n. It's near St. Just. Pretty close to Land's End. Heard of it?'

'I was there in '74 with Yusef. '73 or '74, must've been.'

'Yusef?'

'A Persian – *Iranian* – guy I knew at university.'

Marie coiled her ponytail and pushed in a hairgrip. Her hair was going from auburn to grey. 'You're a dark horse.'

I wasn't sure what she meant by that.

She'd found a holiday cottage on a website and wanted to go ahead and book it for September when the kids had gone back to school and the beaches would be quiet. Not our kids. We'd got over that. But kids in general. Other peoples' kids. She raised an eyebrow.

'He was a mining engineer. He'd had a placement at the Geevor mine for a few weeks. Loved it so much he wanted to go back and dragged me with him.' I was trying to remember a name. 'We camped outside this pub – the Radgel.'

She looked bemused now.

'It's Cornish for fox.'

'And?'

'Can't remember much about it. Great pub. Cornish pasties and beer for breakfast. Nice place. Lots of mining along the coast from what I remember, but that's probably all gone now.'

She was folding the map. 'What kind of mining?'

'Tin. Copper. Mainly tin. Geevor was the last mine to close. There was a big accident there in eighteen-something.'

She looked at me and then back to the map of Cornwall, draining the last of her coffee.

I wanted to get to work. 'Come on, or we'll be late.'

Marie rummaged in her bag for the car keys. I put the breakfast things away and stacked the plates in the dishwasher. It smelled of biriani from the night before. And something else. Something backing up in the drains. I dialled in a hot rinse. Marie was already at the door, pushing her arms into her jacket, lugging her overstuffed briefcase to the car.

*

Yusef standing by the roadside, legs apart. Tight Levi shrink-to-fits. Though mine never did. His cowboy boots are scuffed and he's facing the traffic. Bold as brass. His hair is straight and black, falling across his forehead above jay-feather blue eyes. He cocks his thumb and grins at each driver as they pass. I stand beside him, half a foot shorter in hiking boots and ex-army pants. I've never hitched before. It's seven-thirty in the morning. Cars surf Manchester's rush hour and the early sun melts their windscreens as they move towards us.

Yusef chants his mantra of the road. 'Come on stop, you bastards, give us a break, eh? C'mon baby. C'mon baybee …' Then dipping his thumb ironically as they pass. 'Yeah fuck you, too. Fuck you madam.'

That was Yusef. Easy come, easy go. He didn't mind the endless hanging around trying to bum a ride. He didn't even mind the shite-awful food in trucker's cafes and motorway service stations. I was new to the game and felt vaguely embarrassed at asking for something for nothing. Yusef didn't give a monkey's. 'Man, we are *entitled*!'

His eyes, blue like underwater lapis, crinkle. Now he's racing down the slip road as the first car stops. Slim in his perfectly fitting jeans and Led Zeppelin tee shirt. He has a gold pendant around his neck in the shape of a half moon. He hasn't shaved and his teeth sparkle a grin at the driver from dark stubble. I mean it. They *sparkle*. I watch the smooth brown skin on the nape of his neck as I sit cramped in the back of the car with the rucksacks and tent. Yusef chats to the driver. His father was so rich that they'd once owned a private plane. Then the Shah kicked them out and they'd fled to England. The driver is a pigeon fancier of all things and Yusef is talking to him about racing birds. How does he know this stuff?

The first lift gets us as far as Cannock and dumps us on the M6. Yusef is happy now. He takes a swig of water from the canteen and sprays an arc into the dust. 'Perfect! We'll get down there in a day. Just takes *charisma* ... and balls!' He grins and hoists his crotch. Then he's slapping me on the shoulder, squaring up to the drivers who trundle out from the lorry park, the sun blinding them as they change gear and squint down at us. Miraculously, they stop to pick us up, dazzled by Yusef, who pierces their loneliness. He interrupts their lives of endless driving: service stations, junk food, that solitary early-morning shit with strangers in the next cubicle, dirty roller towels, sleep-overs in the cab, the chance of a woman in a strange town, then sudden, cholesterol-induced death.

*

Marie booked the cottage and we drove down in mid-September, just as planned. Most of the traffic was streaming the other way and we couldn't help feeling smug. It took us three hours to reach Exeter where we did some shopping at the enormous service station and then hit the A30, which runs right down the centre of the peninsula to Land's End, close to where we needed to be. Way past the signs for Jamaica Inn — which rings a sunken bell of memory — we see a sign for Pendeen and I hang a right. The road winds through fields of heather bordered by walls built from huge granite boulders. Ragwort is flowering everywhere. Marie's been dozing but she rouses herself for the last leg. 'It's poisonous.' She's pointing at the hedgerows, splashed with yellow.

'What? Ragwort?'

'Yes. Gorgeous, though.'

There's fuchsia and montbretia and ox-eye daisies nodding in the slipstream of cars. A buzzard slips across the windscreen, wing tips curled upwards as it wheels then rears like a crucifixion. We enter the village almost without noticing we've arrived. I recognise nothing. I feel nothing. The Radgel is still there, at right angles to the road. There's a row of new houses opposite that couldn't have been there when I camped with Yusef. I park the car on the roadside and snap on the handbrake. 'I'd like a pint.'

'I'd like to get there.'

'I know. It's not far.'

'You don't know that.'

'I do, it's close. I've driven all the way. A pint won't kill us will it? C'mon. It's a holiday, remember?'

We climb out of the car, legs stiff from the drive. The sea smells sharp and clean. A line of washing blows about in the back yard of the pub.

The first thing I see in the bar is a black and white photograph of a stout unshaven man in his sixties. *Wally*. The name comes back effortlessly. Wally was the landlord who'd let us pitch our tent in his back field. Yusef had charmed him into it as soon as we arrived. I can't remember how we got there or that final lift, just the hours we spent at Bristol in a queue of other hopefuls. Here's another photograph: five lads in tweed jackets and long hair, two of them with shotguns broken over their arms. They look like they might have been around when we were. A couple of terriers are pulling at their leads and Wally's there again, younger, wearing a collapsed pork-pie hat and a grizzled smile. The same faces looking ten years older are there in the Pendeen cricket team.

Marie's in the loo as I take a quick look round. A thin guy with a ponytail is watching me from behind the bar, drawing on a roll-up. He's got dirt-blue fingernails and Celtic tattoos twining on both arms The pub's familiar in a forgotten sort of way – a long bar with an open fireplace, a back room where we drank with Yusef's tin-mining mates. There's no detail, just a sense of familiar space, vague faces crowding around us.

We take our pints of Tanners outside to where a couple of benches catch the sun. There's a car park beyond and beyond that a small field that looks familiar. Below that the cliffs and the sea. We sit down and Marie gets into conversation with a pleasant looking guy with sandy hair and a generous beer gut. She's friendly like that.

'I was a lifeboat man thirty years, I was. Then my back went. Now I'm a lorry driver. Go all over the place, I do. I saw Britain from the outside from the boat, like, so I reckoned it was time to see the inside. Everywhere from Leominster to Glasgow, Penzance to Manchester. I reckon I must have travelled half way round the world by now. But life on the boats was great. I can't knock it. Not for a moment.'

A wasp hovers above his pint glass, a tiny hyperactive ingot of sun. He whisks it away. His speech sounds rehearsed, as if he's said it a thousand times. I imagine him picking up women as he travels the country, seducing them with his beery breath and easy body.

I leave them to it and walk into the little field. I have to duck under the line of knickers, striped pinnies and babies' nappies. I can just see the lighthouse down to the right on the cliff. It's disused now, but it used to blink in the middle of the night, its rhythmical light slicing the dark. That, at least comes back to me. Groggy with sleep and groping outside the tent to piss. And in the morning, tankers clinging to the blue-grey heat of the horizon. We'd had perfect weather, ten days of sunshine. The only rain had been that night we got smashed on scrumpy.

*

Yusef tossing back his hair and laughing as I try to drive in the tent pegs. They hit stones buried under the soil and bend uselessly. The sun's burned the back of my neck and my tee-shirt's chafing. He drags a little gas stove out of his rucksack humming Stairway to Heaven.

'C'mon Yusef, give me a hand, you're supposed to be a fucking engineer.'

'*Mining* engineer. That's civil engineering, man!' And he's laughing again, his teeth shining, his eyes alert, singing … *and she's buying a stairway to heaven* … another moment of air guitar, then he's holding the ridgepole for me as I tighten a guy line. He smiles. 'Gotta stay cool, Tim.'

'It's too fucking hot to stay cool … it's alright for you.'

He doesn't like that. Frowns. 'What, 'cos I'm Persian? You cunt! I was born in fucking Croydon, man!' And he's laughing again, tossing peanuts into his mouth, necking the pint he's carried from the pub. He pushes back his wristwatch and I see a paler band of skin there under the fine black hairs.

Ginger minge. That's me. The sun brings me out in freckles and sweat. My feet are sticky in my desert boots. I need a wash.

*

The cottage we've hired turns out to be at an awkward corner of the road. We have to park a hundred yards away on the village green and lug our bags. The key's under a bay tree in an earthenware pot in the tiny front garden. The door opens directly into the kitchen. There's a table, a cream coloured Aga that doesn't work any more, an electric cooker, some ramshackle hand-made cupboards and a faint musky smell. The main bedroom and bathroom are downstairs. You can step through French doors from the bedroom to the garden and there's a wooden bench that faces the sea.

Upstairs is the lounge with a large screen TV, a dining table, shelves of romantic novels and some brochures for local restaurants. The owner has left the visitor's book out for us. Marie shrugs, wiping her finger along a shelf to check for dust. 'It's ok, I suppose. I've seen better.'

'It'll do. Bit smelly. Gin?'

I find some ice in the fridge and mix two large G & T's.

Marie puts a couple of Marks & Spencer's lasagnes in the oven and opens a bag of rocket. 'These'll be about twenty minutes.'

I'm setting out two plates and she's smiling at me. Dark green eyes, with pale creases at the corners where the sun's caught her. She takes my arm. 'Come on. Let's try the bed.'

Afterwards we open curtains, clink the ice in our glasses, watch the sun sink over the sea.

*

Yusef twists into a wave on the beach, his body lost in breaking foam. He's shouting me to join him. 'Come on you soft twat!'

A man walking two red setters jerks up his head disapprovingly.

'Come on in!' Yusef laughs, his white teeth perfect as a film star's. I still feel self-conscious about undressing in public. I'm cowering behind a rock, trying to get into my swimming shorts without filling them with sand. Yusef's hair is slicked to his head. He flicks water at me as I tiptoe in. 'C'mon ginger bastard! It's cool.'

'You mean it's fucking freezing!'

Then he's dragging me in. The shock of cold makes me gasp and grab his arm for balance. We stagger into the Atlantic, wave after wave swelling to the shore, sweeping the sand into underwater clouds, knocking the breath from our chests. Our bodies slip against each other. Our mouths are stung by salt. Yusef's skin feels smooth as oil. The gold pendant glitters and bounces on his chest where black hair curls against dark skin.

Afterwards we lie in the sun watching a family of jackdaws squabble on the cliff. There's sand stuck to Yusef's face, tiny glittering particles of quartz. His eyelashes tremble, long and thick. A tanker labours across the horizon, fuming into shades of blue and green. To the south, the leakage of iron oxide stains the sea dark red.

*

The next day, Marie and I drive into St. Just for provisions, wandering past the little art galleries and bric-a-brac shops, drinking morning coffee with the newspapers in a café run by a couple of middle-aged hippies. Middle-aged like us. Old ladies with tattooed arms pass us in the street. They must have been beatniks once. Dreamers, freedom seekers. But whatever you try to get away from follows you. And maybe that's us, invading the peninsula with thousands of others every summer, then leaving them to the winter.

Everyone's friendly and welcoming. Maybe that's just good for business. We buy bread at the bakers and two colossal Cornish pasties, then drive back to the cottage and sit with the ordnance survey map. Marie has her heart set on the coastal path that runs the length of the peninsula and we set off after lunch with a shoulder bag, camera and binoculars, driving to Pendeen, then finding a track that takes us down towards a small bay. We park at a farm, drop a pound coin into the honesty box, then follow a track that winds through gorse thickets and hedgerows tangled with blackberries and rosehips.

The bushes are full of songbirds and the weather is bright with a steady breeze from the sea. Hot gorse releases the scent of coconut as we pass. The old mine workings appear on the cliff top to our left, then the blue curve of the bay begins below. The path crosses over a small stream. I ford it, yards ahead of Marie, and find a notice warning that the beach is full of old metal from shipwrecks and mining. I remember a trickle of blood running from Yusef's heel. *It's nothing man, I didn't even feel it.* His blood seemed unbelievably bright, deeper and redder than any blood I'd seen. Marie's calling from behind. I turn to watch her stumbling over the stream. 'A what?'

'Well you might bloody wait...' She catches up, panting slightly. 'A meadow pipit, I think, could've been a skylark.'

We walk on. Then the beach is there and the Atlantic: green, blue and turquoise, sending cream-topped breakers to the shore. The air is astringent. A family with five kids are making a moated sandcastle where the stream fans over the beach. There are a few walkers on the sand, tiny in the distance. A fat guy tackles the waves on a surfboard, cheered on by his wife and daughters. His shaved head gleams like bronze.

Marie wants to paddle. She always does. Her chest is glazed with sweat, her nipples tight against her tee shirt. The light catches her eyes. 'What's that?' She's pointing above the cliff where a dark shape is hovering. At first it looks like a kestrel, but when I lift the binoculars it has that unmistakeable moustache.

'It's a peregrine!'

Marie's never seen one before. I hand her the binoculars and she fiddles with the focusing wheel.

'Shit! You have them. I can see better without'

I take them back and re-focus. The bird has swooped lower, away from the sun. It's flying into the wind, plumage flustering, tail fanned, wing tips flickering, its breast striated, its body rocking on the air. Its head is fiercely alert, gimbaling from side to side. It slackens and sinks lower, trembling in the streaming air. It folds its wings and dives, swooping into bracken. Marie is touching my arm. 'It's got something!'

'Yeah, a meadow pipit, probably.'

She slaps my elbow and the bird rises again, steering away down coast.

We walk barefoot at the edge of the sea, letting the waves wet our trouser hems. Afterwards we pull on our walking shoes and follow the coastal path up through the cliff, a circular route that winds to the Levant mine through heather and granite, then back to the village.

By six o'clock we're outside the Radgel rubbing cream into our arms and drinking bitter shandies. Then a tedious last mile to the car, our feet aching against hot tarmac. Before we leave, Marie pulls a plastic bag out of the boot and we pick blackberries, feeling for the fruit amongst the briars and nettles that have grown into the hawthorn hedge, pricking our fingers and staining them with juice. I remember my mother telling me how she'd picked rosehips in the war to make jelly for the soldiers in the hospital where she was a nurse. I'd taken her blackberries and stewed apples a few days before she died, spooning them into her mouth.

Marie and I drive back to the cottage in sun-stunned silence, watching robins and wrens break from the hedgerows, then shadows stretching from the pithead wheel.

There's a bottle of Australian Chardonnay cooling in the fridge. We open it after taking showers in the cramped bathroom. We make love. We doze, then wake to the dark, to half empty glasses beside the bed. A thrush is singing outside in short, cascading phrases. Marie stirs and kisses my chest. Her hot breath sighs across my skin but I can't tell whether that's longing or satisfaction.

*

On the last day we hitch to the Blue Anchor at Helstone to try the beer they brewed on the premises. A young clergyman picks us up in an ancient split-windscreen Morris Minor. I sit in the back as usual, whilst Yusef fields his questions. There's a Welsh Springer behind me, asleep on an old blanket. The dog farts, filling the car with the stench of rotten meat. The clergyman chuckles and winds down a window. 'Sorry gents. Don't mind Waffles.'

I see Yusef frown. He doesn't do dogs. He turns to me behind the clergyman's back, making his fingers into a gun and pointing them towards the Springer. We don't speak much after that until the vicar drops us off.

In the Blue Anchor we drink four pints of the dark bitter that's brewed on the premises and then reel out into the light. The sun is blinding. Yusef blinks theatrically. 'Fuck, that was *schtrong*.'

Yusef has spotted a good hitching point on the way in, where there's a broad verge beside the road. We walk into open country and start to thumb. Progress is slow. We end up climbing over a gate to piss against the hedge. I start to feel slightly nauseous in the heat, the beer dragging at my belly. The sun's blistering my face and my nose is peeling. We don't reach Pendeen until gone six. When we get into the bar of the Radgel, Yusef's greeted noisily by some of his mining chums. We feel great. Triumphant.

Hours later, and before I realise it, we've switched from beer to scrumpy. I remember Wally going into the back room, emerging with the dregs of the barrel. Two pints of scummy pink froth. The broken-toothed grin of Beaky saying something dirty in his clotted Cornish accent, so close I can smell his armpits. Yusef's chuckling. The room is dense with laughter and blue cigarette smoke. I want to heave, but hang on as everything dissolves. The room turning on its lost moments like a fairground ride. We're drinking sour candy floss. Then, mysteriously, we're out in the Atlantic rain, struggling with the zip of the tent. We stagger in the mud. Laughing, cursing. Nylon cracks in the wind. Then a voice mutters inside the tent, which isn't ours. *Fuckfuckfuckit.* This one has a zip that runs round the edge. Ours has a centre zip. Clawing our way through rain, we find our tent behind. Then I'm throwing up into the rain, the lighthouse blinking, Yusef's hand on my neck.

Somehow there's a fight with clothes and sleeping bags. I'm sipping water from the plastic bottle, pissing in the rain, dragging off my wet tee shirt. Body heat. The sweet sharpness of sweat. Yusef's skin smooth against mine. He's laughing, his lips against my neck, his body arched above me. My hands feel his spine, his hips, the curve of his arse. I've still got my socks on and reach down to take them off, but Yusef gets there first, pulling them over my feet. The taste of salt. My face hot. Sleep. Then waking in a tangle of clothes, rucksacks pushed against the side of the tent where they've let rain percolate. Yusef naked on his back, his pubic bush gleaming, his cock limp against his thigh. Faint snail trails have dried there on his skin. He smells of marzipan and bleach and beer all mixed together. I dress quickly, crouching, careful not to wake him, though he might already be awake. I step outside onto wet grass in startling sunshine. The couple in the tent in front of us are making breakfast. The smell of bacon frying brings Yusef to the door of the tent, growling with a hangover, tousled, but flashing his best smile at the couple who make us both a cup of tea.

*

Every day we choose a different route to walk, sometimes taking lunch, sometimes stopping off at a pub. We see Cape Cornwall, Land's End, Sennen Bay, Porthcurno, Mousehole, Carn Goose Promontary and those tiny islands, the Brisons, where cormorants are crowded together to dry their wings against a glittering sea. We swim on the beach below the Monnack Theatre and doze on a strip of white sand. In the evenings, I cook or we go to a restaurant. In the mornings we wake and I make tea in the little kitchen, enjoying the early morning scent of gas, the feeling of being alone before the day begins. After dinner, we watch the sun from the upstairs lounge, going down through torn cinema curtains to the sea where the tankers tack backwards and forwards. We stew the blackberries and keep them in the fridge, adding a dab of clotted cream. We read in the evening, then lie with clasped hands each night listening to last traffic on the road that runs past the house to Land's End before we sink into sleep.

One day we find Priest's Cove, making our way down past lobster pots and floats and beached fishing boats to the concrete jetty. The beach is formed from smooth boulders, mysterious as blank skulls. Three elderly ladies are getting into their swimming costumes. They flip-flop to the sea, splashing their shoulders, sculling towards sunset, their arms breaking its tilting mirrors. Walking home, we find campion bobbing in the wind.

*

For two days Yusuf hardly spoke. When we headed north again he didn't carry his shoulders with the same swagger and left me to do the hitching. We came most of the way home in a furniture van, driving through the night, side by side on the bench seat, our legs touching, a yellow cheese of moon looming over Somerset. When we got to Manchester, the city was still asleep. We said goodbye in Piccadilly Square, under the statue of Queen Victoria. Yusef swung his arm and let his fist hit me lightly on the mouth. Not a real blow, but real enough.

'See you Ginge.'

I was too stunned to speak, lips stinging from his fist. He turned away, hoisting his rucksack, his heels striking the paving stones. He looked over his shoulder and smiled and said again. 'See you.'

But I didn't see him. We went our separate ways and I never saw him again. I heard that he'd gone to Manitoba to mine copper. But maybe that was just a rumour. When I got home and washed my clothes, I found his pendant stuffed into the pocket of the spare jeans in my rucksack. I wonder where in the world he is now.

*

Marie and I went home on the Saturday. As I flung the junk mail down the hallway, she touched me on the temple, brushing back my hair. She looked as if she was about to cry. 'I love you, you know. Whatever you might think.'

I didn't know what to say. We'd had a good week, but we'd driven home in silence. Something had thickened around us and it wasn't just sadness at our holiday coming to an end. Maybe it was the lives we could have led. I don't know. Yusef's pendant pressed into my chest where it was buttoned into the pocket of my shirt. Why did she say that?

I piled up the mail, watched the answer-phone blinking, switched on the kettle as Marie pushed the kitchen windows open. The house was chilly with absence. I carried our bags upstairs and placed them side-by-side on the bed, ready to unpack.

The Dahlia Bed

Helen Dunmore

Nina watched the black dahlia across the bald, baked stretch of Corporation grass. She hadn't brought anything to lie on and the ground was rougher than it looked. She rolled onto her stomach and watched red ants make their way in and out of the thick grass stems. Every so often she would stretch out. The pressure of the sun weighed her down.

Holiday time. She propped her chin on her hands and squinted uphill towards the dahlia bed. No park in England had a richer variety of species. On a notice behind glass it said that the Corporation had won a bronze award in the International Dahlia Festival, judged by a visiting delegation from Holland.

'Holland,' thought Nina. She saw a boy bicycling endlessly along the top of a dyke, pressed between a heavy sky and broad, flooding waters. 'Why Holland?' Those judges must have had a shock when they got to the dahlia bed. All this city around them, dark and swarming. The bold, cynical looks people had on their faces. They'd have given it bronze, just to get away safely. She remembered driving into the city for the first time, two years ago, when she was fourteen. The road ran between fields which had the marred look of being too near a city. Cooling towers reared to the left of them. Her father's lips were tight, as if he thought this was what they all deserved. Nina sat in the back seat with her little brother on her lap.

It was Saturday and there was a match on. They slowed as thousands of men poured out of the gates and across the road, filling it because they had the right of numbers. They didn't hurry themselves. All their caps seemed set in the same direction, but no, men were parting, dividing, going home this way and that. She saw one or two faces touched by a look of grim satisfaction, but most were blank. A few lads yelled to one another. The team had lost and there was no colour anywhere.

The men pushed their way around the car, their weight rocking it a little. Nina listened to her parents as they opened out the map so it filled the front of the car, and tried to find the way through the centre of the city. They had bought a house and now they were looking for it. Nina felt a familiar stab of hope, of familial eagerness that soon, any moment now, a good time would begin. Her father would get out at a newsagent's with no explanation and come back with cigarettes for himself and a white paper bag which he would toss into the back of the car. Inside it there would be Mars bars, Maltesers and a bar of Cadbury's Fruit and Nut. She could remember in her body the fizz of bliss that he used to conjure on days out at the sea. Even out of loyalty, she couldn't summon it now.

They should never have turned off the Great North Road. They should have driven on until they came to the Roman Wall, and then dropped down the few miles to the Tyne. They could have parked the car outside the house, by the beech hedge. Nina would have said, 'I'll go and open the door,' and taken the Yale off her mother's palm. There might have been an awkward moment when her former self just stared at her, wide-eyed and astonished, but then she would have slipped easily into her old body and rushed out to show the others what they had to become. Even her wriggling, shouting little brother would soon settle down into the old black pram under the rowan tree. He would understand that he was a baby again, and look up at the leaves while he turned his fists against the light.

Now they were leaving again. The house was sold to a builder who planned to build a second house in the garden. Nina would give something to see that garden obliterated, with its shameful corners peeped into by all the hungry eyes from the old people's home next door.

They were going, but this time she wasn't going with them. She was too old now to be crammed into the back of a car with the little ones and driven a hundred miles to the next home. She had found a bedsit and she would get a job.

Hundreds of yards of dahlias. Each autumn they were taken in before the first frosts could turn them to slime in the ground. Nina had seen the gardeners at their task, easing tubers out of the earth, shaking them clean. They labelled each bundle before putting in into a sack on a wheelbarrow.

In a few more weeks the gardeners would come for the dahlias again. By the time they were out of the earth, she would be on her own.

The black dahlia pulled her to her feet and brought her to the shabby edge of the grass. All the life of the park, all its money and effort, was in the dahlias. The trees were unkempt and the bandstand had no band. The corporation did not care, as long as the park had its dahlia bed. Nina could almost smell the obsession. Bronze would never be enough. Next time the Dutch would be held hostage until they gave the gold.

As she came closer she saw that the flower was not really black. Its hollow petals were purplish bronze. There was sticky nectar at the centre of the flowers, where flies struggled. Nina stared up the long dahlia border. Names were written on plastic labels and thrust into the earth, but at this time of year they were hidden by leaves and glaring flowers.

The flies which had not yet become trapped moved about in a cloud, simmering among the oranges and pinks. The flowers had no scent but there was something rank in the air. Their leaves, perhaps. There were dahlias like buttons, and big ragged flowers that aped chrysanthemums.

An old man stooped his way down the border. He wore a trilby hat and he poked his stick in among the flowers. His skin had an ashen bloom. He pushed back his hat and examined a wide, gaping, scarlet flower. He reached out and turned the flower's head until it stared straight at him. So brazen – no wonder his face was severe. He let the flower drop, with a touch of contempt. She wondered if the Dutch had adjudicated as ruthlessly. He made a sound of dismissal with his teeth, then he caught Nina's eyes and grimaced as if they were two parents watching the unappealing antics of a stranger's child.

'Give me a flower that is a flower.' His voice creaked and bubbled, but there was still strength in it. He was very old, she realised. What she could see of his hair was white. 'Give

me a rose,' he went on in a commanding tone. 'Smell a rose
and you feel it down to the soles of your shoes.'

As he spoke she felt wet, sweet petals brush against
her lips. The clusters of white and cream roses that fell over
the back wall in a house they'd lived in for a while when she
was five or six. Where the house was she couldn't remember.
But the startle of that rose went all the way through her body.
There was another one, blackish crimson and too heavy for its
stem. It would fill up with rain and then bow down. She would
reach up and turn the black rose over with slow, shivering
greed, knowing what was coming. She always shut her eyes.

'These are dead-hearted flowers,' said the man.

The ice-cream van began to jingle. Just a few notes, up
and down, and then the van's engine started up again. The sun
had faded behind a yellow veil of petrol fumes. Soon the air
would begin to move, languidly at first and then enough to
whip up the ice-cream wrappers and dead leaves.

'Each day I come to this park. Each day,' said the
man.

Now Nina was sure that he was addressing her. 'I
come sometimes,' she said.

The man nodded, pressing his lips together. 'You like
them? You like these things?' he demanded, gesturing at the
dahlias.

Nina followed his gaze. There were yellow pom-poms
and single flowers that looked like anemones. Behind them
were huge staggering flowers, propped up on sticks. They
lolled out into the exhausted air like wolves' tongues. She
would have been fine if the man hadn't spoken to her, but
because he looked into her face and asked her a question, she
wanted to cry. The afternoon was like a black dahlia. She was a
fly treading her feet in the treacly heart of it. She couldn't free
herself.

'Not much,' said Nina, and the man laughed silently.
After a while he nodded as if he'd had enough. He walked
along the border, inspecting it, lifting his stick high so that for
a second Nina thought he would slash the faces off the dead-
hearted flowers. The wind was beginning to move and her
dress was loose against her body. She could not think what to
do next.

The man was back. 'You come here every day, you see everyone,' he informed her. 'Rosie O'Mahoney, Mrs Siddons, John the Baptist.'

Nina came out of her dream. Her eyes narrowed. The man gave a rich crack of laughter.

'Don't you read the labels?' he demanded.

'Oh!' He was saying the names of the dahlias, that was all.

'You thinking I lost my mind, seeing John the Baptist in the park? Is that it?'

She blushed and looked down.

'You should read the labels. You a student?'

Nina shook her head.

'You still at school?'

'No.'

'You should study. You should get information.' The man rapped his stick on the path to reinforce his point. Then he sighed, looking down the Corporation lawn at the picnickers. Nina heard the wheeze in his chest.

'Give me a rose any day,' he said. 'You should study. You doing no good to yourself here. Summer be gone soon.'

Summer be gone soon. The words fell on her ears like rain. The park would be empty, or crossed by people walking the paths briskly, pulling their coats around them. Nina smiled in huge relief. None of this mattered. It would all be gone soon, swept away by rain and the smell of bonfire smoke. If she was alone it didn't matter. Swiftly, she looked to the left and the right before stepping onto the dry crust of the flower-bed. There was the black dahlia. There was its label, thrust into the ground and hidden by leaves. She bent down.

'It's called James Ellroy,' she said aloud.

'James Ellroy,' the man repeated.

Nina stepped back onto the grass. The man rubbed out her footprints with the end of his stick. 'Now you got your information,' he said.

Autumn was coming. Everything would soon be starting again.

'I can get you James Ellroy,' said the man, looking into her face. Nina did not know what answer he wanted.

'All right,' she said at last.

Nimbly, in what looked like one movement, the man stepped into the flower-bed. He weighed the black dahlia in his hand and then snapped the stem. He stepped back and again removed the footprints with his stick. He gave the flower to Nina. He nodded at her, his face stern, and then he looked all around him before he walked away with purpose, not even glancing at the dahlia bed.

She lifted the flower to her lips. She drew in the sharp scent of a chrysanthemum, bronze and cold, set like a jewel in a bed of frost.

Writers

Rachel Bentham has written many radio dramas and short stories for BBC Radio 4 and is an internationally published poet. She lives in Bristol with three of her children and two dogs. Currently, she's finishing a novel set in nineteenth century Tahiti about a woman with 'murderer' tattooed on her face.

Krishan Coupland was born in Southampton, England, and now studies at Staffordshire University. His work has appeared in Brittle Star, Aesthetica, and 3AM Magazine.

Philippa de Burlet*'s* career highlights include train cleaner, zookeeper, artist and art teacher. She currently has a 'proper job' in arts education (paid holidays) and she makes things. She began to write stories a while back and is now working on a novel, a gay historical romance with clotted cream and Devonshire dialect.

Mark Czanik*'s* poems and short stories have appeared widely in magazines, most recently Planet, Wasafiri, Staple, Blue Tattoo, and Cyphers. He lives in Bath with his wife and daughter, where, between writing, he currently works as a gardener on a crazy golf course and as a receptionist at a tennis club.

Jane Draycott was named as one of the PBS 'Next Generation' poets 2004 and was a recent Stephen Spender Prize-winner for her new translation of the medieval dream-vision *Pearl*, due from Carcanet Oxford Poets in 2010. Her most recent poetry collection *Over* is published by Carcanet Oxford Poets (2009).

Helen Dunmore is a novelist, poet, short-story and children's writer. She has published three collections of short stories, *Love of Fat Men*, *Ice Cream* and *Rose, 1944*. Among other awards, her work has received the Orange Prize for Fiction and the McKitterick Prize. She is a fellow of the Royal Society of Literature.

David Gaffney is the author of *Sawn Off Tales* (Salt 2006), *Aromabingo* (Salt 2007), *Never Never* (Tindal Street 2008), *Buildings Crying Out* (Lancaster litfest 2009), *23 Stops To Hull* (Humbermouth festival 2009) *Rivers Take Them* a set of short operas with composer Ailis Ni Riain (BBC Radio Three 2008.) and *Destroy PowerPoint*, (Edinburgh Festival Fringe 2009) *www.davidgaffney.co.uk*

Jane Feaver is author of *According to Ruth* (Harvill Secker, 2007) and *Love Me Tender* (Harvill Secker, 2009), an interlinked collection of short stories set in North Devon. She is currently at work on a third novel and studying for a PhD at Exeter University.

Michael Owen Fisher is a 30-year-old writer living in Brighton. He has worked as a researcher and a teacher, and this year is writing his first novel 'How to Catch a Cold'.

Nicholas Hogg was born in Leicester. After graduating from the University of East London with a psychology degree, he travelled widely, living in Japan, Fiji and America. Winner of the New Writing Ventures prize for fiction in 2005, and twice short-listed for the Eric Gregory award for young poets, Canongate published his first novel *Show me the Sky* in 2008 to tremendous acclaim.

Eleanor Knight has recently moved to Lewes where, if she doesn't finish a novel soon, something terrible will happen. Her stories have appeared in the Serpent's Tail anthology Retro Retro and Riptide Vol. 2. She has written about the nuclear warning system for the *Independent* and linoleum for *Elle Decoration*.

Anna Lunk is a Creative Writing and Literature tutor based in Totnes. Many of her short stories are 'site specific' – written for performance. She is currently working on a novel examining the dilemmas facing a recently retired camerawoman who has devoted her life to the pursuit of beauty.

Graham Mort teaches creative writing at Lancaster University and has worked extensively in Africa for the British Council on literature development and radio broadcast projects. His latest book - *Visibility: New & Selected Poems* was published by Seren in 2007, when he also won the Bridport prize for short fiction. A book of short stories - *Touch* - will appear from Seren in 2010.

Kachi A. Ozumba is a winner of the Decibel Penguin Short Story Prize and the Commonwealth Short Story Prize. He holds an MA (Distinction) in Creative Writing from the University of Leeds. His short stories have been broadcast and published by the BBC, and have appeared in many journals and anthologies. His debut novel, *The Shadow of a Smile,* is due out in September 2009.

Gemma Rutter is a Creative Writing graduate, who writes furiously and often, as a journalist, poet, and aspiring novelist. Gemma has previously been published in Safari Young Poets, The Cadaverine Magazine, Creature Magazine and Random Acts of Writing. She is Consulting Editor of The Cadaverine Magazine.

Anita Sivakumaran is hacking a novel about the hysteria and moral squalor of the ambitious people in glamorous professions in urban India. This is her second novel; the first one is buried deep in an undisclosed location.

Henry Shukman has won the Author's Club First Novel Award, an Arts Council Writer's Award, and been a finalist for the O. Henry Prize. Both *Darien Dogs* (Cape, 2004) and *The Lost City* (Little Brown, 2007) were *Guardian* Books of the Year. As a poet he won the Jerwood Aldeburgh Poetry Prize for his first collection, *In Dr No's Garden* (Cape 2002), which was also a Book of the Year in the *Times* (London) and *Guardian*.

Joel Willans was born in Suffolk and now works as a copywriter for a Helsinki ad agency. His fiction has been broadcast on BBC Radio, and published in many anthologies and magazines including Penumbra, Brand, Pen Pusher, Flash, Southword, Route and The Momaya Review. In 2008, he won the Yeovil Literary Prize and Global Short Story Award.

Cover Illustration

Matt Thomas lives and works in rural Devon. He uses traditional as well as found, natural materials to create abstract pictures inspired by and set in the area between Exmoor and Dartmoor. 'Grey Summer Sky' has been reproduced from a monoprint with pastel and yellow clay. E-mail contact: *evanonrev@yahoo.co.uk*